GHOSTWRITER

Sarah reached around to the back of her computer and switched it off. She watched the letters fade, but as the screen grew dark the strange reflection began to reappear. She could see it clearly now. Someone was staring back at her from the computer screen—a young girl with dark, anxious, pleading eyes.

The Ghost
Inside the Monitor

Margaret J. Anderson

Bullseye Books · Alfred A. Knopf
New York

A BULLSEYE BOOK PUBLISHED BY ALFRED A. KNOPF, INC.

Library of Congress Cataloging-in-Publication Data
Anderson, Margaret Jean.
The ghost inside the monitor by Margaret J. Anderson.
p. cm.
Summary: While working in her father's computer store,
eleven-year-old Sarah finds a terminal containing the ghost of a young
girl who lived in the area in the early years of the century,
and the connection pulls her through the computer into that
other girl's time period.
[1. Time travel—Fiction.   2. Computers—Fiction.]   I. Title.
PZ7.A54397Gh   1990   [Fic]—dc20   89-26848   CIP   AC
ISBN: 0-679-80359-9 (pbk.)   0-679-90359-3 (lib. bdg.)
RL: 5.1
First Bullseye Books edition: September 1990

Manufactured in the United States of America
1   2   3   4   5   6   7   8   9   10

for Alex, Judith, and Bob

—M. A.

I

The Big Apple

Sarah Pearce stared moodily out the window into the twisted branches of the huge oak tree that shaded the south side of the apartment building. She tuned out her mom telling her that breakfast was on the table. This was going to be the longest summer in her entire life. The longest summer in all her eleven years.

The Pearces had just moved from California to Oregon. Sarah didn't know a single person in Dixon Landing outside her own family. And she didn't see how she was ever going to meet anyone. She was the only child in the apartment building. The manager had made it plain that he didn't care for kids, but her parents had assured him that Sarah was exceptionally quiet and wouldn't cause any trouble. Her dad liked the idea of living close to downtown, where he'd just opened a computer store in the new Dewey Shopping Plaza. Her mom liked the apartment because it was small and full of labor-saving devices. She was starting her master's degree in child psychology at Dixon

College, and now that she was a student again she didn't have time for housework. Her thesis was on how children react to new situations in their lives. Sarah hoped she wasn't going to end up as a case history.

"Come and have breakfast, Sarah!" her mom repeated briskly. "We're running late."

Sarah refrained from pointing out that she, personally, had nothing to run late for. Instead she slid into her chair and asked—not for the first time—"Why can't I go back to Menlo Park and stay with Tina? Just till school starts."

Her mom suppressed a sigh. "Give it a chance, Sarah. You'll make friends here pretty soon."

Her dad lowered his newspaper. "Want to come down to the store this morning? I could use some low-paid help."

"I guess so," Sarah said grudgingly, reaching for a muffin. "I don't have anything better to do."

"I've been thinking about starting a computer club like the one we had in Menlo Park. On Saturday mornings, before the store opens at ten. What do you think, Sarah?"

"Are you sure you'd want a bunch of people messing around with your computers?"

"We'd get along fine," Mr. Pearce said confidently. "And it would be good advertising. Who knows, some of the kids might nag their parents into buying them one of their own! Besides, it would be a way for you to make some friends."

Sarah shrugged. The kids who'd hung around the computer store in Menlo Park had all been machine-oriented. They'd been tuned in to programs, not people. It wouldn't be any different here.

The Dewey Shopping Plaza was very modern compared with the rest of downtown—all stained wood and dark glass and odd angles, so that it was hard to see how the stores fit together inside. In the middle of the paved plaza rose a fountain—a tall, fluted column with water bubbling out the top and dribbling down the sides instead of spraying out the way a fountain should. Inside the building the shops were on different levels connected by ramps. The Book Nook and two clothing stores—Denim Blues and Underthings Unlimited—were on the ground level. Then there was a jewelry store and a greeting-card shop. Around the next curve across from the Double Scoop was the Big Apple. Through the windows facing the ramp you could see the computers separated from one another by low partitions. Mr. Pearce believed in a hands-on approach so that customers could compare different models and programs for themselves.

Sarah sniffed the new-building smell while she waited for her dad to unlock the door. Then she followed him inside. A huge bunch of flowers left over from the grand opening just last Saturday stood against the counter. They were arranged to match the rainbow colors of the Apple.

"You can start by bringing the inventory disk up to date, Sarah," Mr. Pearce suggested. "I haven't entered that new shipment of game programs. And count how many boxes of computer paper we have in the back room, and how many printer ribbons. Be sure to get all the ordering codes right."

After Sarah had counted the boxes and checked them off on a list, she came back out to the store to enter the numbers on the computer. Before she switched it on, she could see her face in the dark screen, but there was something odd about the lighting in the store. Her reflection didn't look right. Sarah had a round face and straight brown hair with bangs across her forehead. Her worst feature was her ears: they stuck out through her hair—unless she pushed her hair behind them, and then they looked even bigger. The person looking out of the computer seemed to have curly dark hair that hid her ears and a pointed chin.

Sarah moved her head to the side. The face was still there in the middle of the screen, but the eyes followed her. Weird!

Feeling a little uneasy, she hurriedly loaded the inventory disk. The reflection was lost as the green lettering appeared, but the letters were fuzzy. Each one had a little ghost beside it.

"This is hard to read, Dad," she complained.

"It looks all right to me," Mr. Pearce answered, leaning over Sarah's shoulder.

And it did look all right now.

Sarah began to enter the numbers while her dad designed a notice for his Saturday computer club on a Macintosh. Mr. Pearce didn't believe in letting ideas get away from him. When he'd finished, he taped the notice to the glass front door, so that anyone entering the store would see it.

About fifteen minutes later, Sarah looked up from the computer when the first customer of the day walked in. She did a quick inventory on him. Male, around twelve, reddish hair that stuck up in front, nervous blue eyes that darted from one computer to the next, faded jeans, a green soccer shirt.

The rainbow bouquet began to rock, and the boy grabbed it to steady it, though Sarah didn't think he had bumped it. On second thought he must have, because there was no one else near it.

"Anything I can help you with?" Mr. Pearce asked. His voice was friendly, but he didn't come out from behind the counter. He wasn't expecting to make a big sale.

"Well . . . I was just looking . . ." the boy said.

Sarah added braces to her mental inventory.

The boy sidled over to the rack of game disks.

"Did you see the notice about the computer club I'm starting?" Mr. Pearce asked.

"I took a computer class at school last year," the

boy said eagerly. "I'd like to sign up—if it doesn't cost too much."

"You have to supply your own disk. That'll run about two dollars. Beyond that, it's free."

"Would you put my name down? Jeff Cuff."

"I'd be glad to. I'm Tom Pearce and this is Sarah."

Jeff watched Mr. Pearce write down his name and then he headed for the door.

"See you on Saturday, Jeff!" Mr. Pearce called after him. "Around eight."

"Yes, sir! Thank you, sir!"

As the door closed Sarah's dad winked at her and circled his thumb and first finger into an OKAY sign. Sarah glowered at the screen. Her dad didn't need to act as though he were running a computer dating service.

2

Dixon Landing

After Sarah finished the inventory, she slipped Applewriter into the disk drive. She liked to write—anything—stories, poems, even reports for school. Especially on a computer. She was planning to write her autobiography, starting with the present and working back. With a word processor she could rearrange chapters later, so it didn't much matter where she began.

She typed the heading: COMING TO DIXON LANDING.

Then she leaned back in her chair, thinking about the day she'd left Menlo Park. Tina had come over with a good-bye present—a little blue stuffed dolphin. She and Tina had done a report together at school on dolphins and had given a demonstration on "dolphin talk," whistling to each other. From where Sarah was sitting she could see her reflection on the screen. She was getting a little misty-eyed thinking about the good old days with Tina, which might account for the fact that she didn't look like herself again. She bent forward for a closer look, but the face faded, leaving the screen blank except for the heading.

Feeling vaguely unsettled, Sarah began to write about the trip from California. How her mom had driven the car and her dad the U-Haul truck with all their stuff. It had been a long, boring journey up the freeway. Her account of it was boring, too. Short and boring. She'd been asleep when they'd reached Dixon Landing, so she couldn't record her first impressions of her new hometown. Maybe she ought to start her autobiography with a more exciting episode from her life. She stared at the screen, at a loss where to begin—and not because there were too many exciting events to choose from.

While she was waiting for inspiration, the account of her trip suddenly vanished, as if a momentary power loss had cleared the screen. But the heading was still there, and even stranger than that, new words were appearing on the monitor, one letter at a time. Sarah's fingers weren't anywhere near the keyboard. She watched, fascinated, as the computer typed in an entry all by itself.

When Sarah read the words, she was astonished to find that they made sense. A story had actually written itself, letter by letter, word by word. A story that matched the title but had nothing to do with her or her family's move from California.

COMING TO DIXON LANDING

I remember the journey from Salem to Dixon Landing as if it were yesterday. We were traveling on the steamship *Grahamona*. It was late in the year and the Willamette River was in flood. Instead of looking out on woods and fields and farms I saw nothing but brown water under a leaden sky.

The river had spilled over its banks to form a lake, an ocean, turning clumps of trees into islands. Fences and fields and sheds were under water. Standing on the deck in the pelting rain, looking out over the rail, I caught sight of only one living creature all afternoon—a farm dog. For a while he followed us, running along the edge of the water. I could tell he was barking, but he was so far away that the sound didn't reach us. He splashed into the water and then retreated. Finally he gave up and turned and walked dejectedly away. I went inside, feeling sorry for the dog, though at that time I didn't know how awful it is to reach out to people and have them refuse to see you.

Mama and Papa sang with the Opera Company, performing in the small towns up and down the valley. During those long, slow journeys on the Willamette River they often played with me and sang and told me stories. Sometimes they were learning their parts for the next show, but I always imagined they were doing it for me. Or the whole cast of the Opera would perform for the other passengers, and then I would sit near the front, puffed up with pride because the beautiful leading lady was my mama. She had thick chestnut hair, bright eyes, and red, red lips. Everyone loved Maria Jouet.

But there was no singing and laughter on that trip. And not just because of the weather. Mama was ill. She lay huddled in her cloak on one of the red plush seats in the lounge, her chestnut hair straggly and dark with sweat. Her eyes were far away. She hardly seemed to see me crouched at her side. Between bouts of coughing she called out for Papa. I finally went looking for him, but he wouldn't come. He was helping Clara Whitehorn learn her lines. To me they sounded like Mama's lines, and that made me angry.

By the time Sarah had read the entry through to the end, she felt annoyed as well as bewildered. The computer's story was far more interesting than hers! But thinking it over, Sarah decided it didn't really make sense after all. There were no steamships on the Willamette River. If you were going from Salem to Dixon Landing you came down Interstate 5. Though people could have traveled by steamship long ago. The writing sounded old-fashioned. Nobody Sarah knew called their parents Mama and Papa. And what did that mean about it being awful to reach out to people and have them refuse to see you?

Sarah started to call her dad over to take a look at the story on the screen, but she stopped herself. He was demonstrating a computer in the next booth to Ben, their new technician, and she could tell from the way he was hunched close to the screen that they had some kind of problem. So she hit the print key. She could show him the story later.

When the words on the screen began to appear on paper, Sarah felt surprised all over again, even though that was what you'd expect to happen when you hit the print key. By the time the printer stopped, she had so many questions that she snatched the pages from the machine and charged into the next booth without waiting for her dad to finish with Ben.

"Take a look at this, Dad!" she said breathlessly.

As her dad reached for the paper a sudden burst of static came from somewhere behind the computer and all the store lights flickered. The screen glowed for a second and then went dark. Mr. Pearce muttered under his breath, while Ben quickly unplugged the computer.

This was definitely not the time to confront them with another problem.

"I'll let you see this some other time, Dad," Sarah said, retreating.

Mr. Pearce nodded absent-mindedly. After booting up the machine, he replaced the disk.

Sarah's computer screen was blank, too. Probably because of the power surge.

But then she recalled the strange wistful reflection. And the entry that wrote itself. And the burst of static. Three unconnected events.

Or were they?

She spent the rest of the morning carefully copying the story from the printout onto the computer. When she was finished, she saved it on a brand-new disk under the file name MYSTERY.

At noon, when Sarah went home to the empty apartment to fix her own lunch, she took the story along with her even though she practically knew it by heart. Her dad had already forgotten that she had something to show him, but she didn't care. He'd have come up with some electronic explanation that wouldn't really answer anything. She liked things better the way they were—her mystery and her secret.

3

My New Home

The next day Sarah's autobiography changed itself again. This time she was describing the apartment. She called the entry MY NEW HOME. She had written that what she liked best about their apartment was the way it was shaded by a huge oak tree. When she sat on the little balcony that opened off the dining room, it was almost like being in a tree house. But that didn't make up for having no yard. The living room, which opened into the dining room—every room opened into another room—had a dark red couch with a black-and-white woodblock print of two sea gulls on the wall behind it. On the coffee table was a china bowl filled with blue and yellow pansies. Even the pansies were made out of china.

Sarah was trying to think of what to write next when she felt a cold draft at the back of her neck. She looked around to see if a customer had left the door open. By the time she turned back, her description of the apartment was gone. A completely different story was appearing on the screen.

MY NEW HOME

I'd been to Dixon Landing before, but that evening the town was different from my memory of it. It's that way with places you've seen only in summer and then return to in the wintertime. The *Grahamona* had to dock at a makeshift wharf because the river was so high. Dixon Landing looked bleak and uninviting. I hoped we wouldn't be staying long.

First and Second streets were under water. We crossed them on planks perched on wooden barrels. Papa and Mama and I didn't go to the hotel with the rest of the Opera Company. Instead we went to the Dewey House on Baker Street near the edge of town, where Papa had arranged for rooms. Because Mama was sick, I suppose.

It was a big house with a front porch. A heavy-set man in a dark suit opened the door and told us to step inside. He introduced himself as Alfred Jardine. His wife, Maud, came out of a room on the left to greet us. We stood in the hall, our coats and bags dripping from the rain. Maud Jardine was a tall woman dressed in a blue silk gown with a stiff lace collar that seemed to push her chin into the air. Her hair was piled on top of her head, making her look even taller.

"I didn't know there was a child!"

"She'll be no trouble," Papa assured her. "She's very quiet and is used to amusing herself."

Mrs. Jardine looked down at me from her great height as if I were some creature that Mama and Papa had fished out of the river. The fact that my boots and the bottom of my dress were muddy and that water was dripping from my cape, my hair, and even from the tip of my nose must have made this seem possible. To make matters worse, a boy was standing behind the woman, pulling faces at me. He was a year or two older than I was and had big front teeth like a beaver.

Mama began to cough, leaning heavily against Papa.

I half expected the stone-faced woman to tell us to go away, but she turned to Mama and said, quite kindly, "You'd better get out of that wet coat. Come into the kitchen where there's a fire."

I would have followed them, but she stopped me, saying, "My sister Tibbie will see to you!"

It was then that I noticed another woman hovering in the shadows. Tibbie was around twenty, but because I was only eight she seemed quite old. I could see right away that she was different from her sister—the way a sparrow is different from a blue jay. She wore a big apron over her plain brown wool dress, and she beckoned to me timidly. Although I didn't want to leave Mama and Papa, I followed her upstairs.

She took me to a room at the back of the house. It was nicer than any room I'd ever been in before. The window was framed with ruffled curtains, and the red and pink roses with interwoven stems on the wallpaper looked so real that you could almost smell them. Though perhaps the perfume came from the jars of rose petals and lavender on the chest of drawers. The bed was covered with a colorful patchwork quilt.

"It's pretty," I whispered.

"There's water in the ewer," Miss Tibbie said, pointing to a heavy pitcher sitting in a basin. "Get yourself cleaned up. I'll be back in a minute."

When Miss Tibbie left, I wanted to run downstairs again to find Mama and Papa, but I was afraid of that Mrs. Jardine. Now the water running down my cheeks was tears instead of rain.

I was still standing in the same place when Miss Tibbie came back. She was carrying a doll with a china face and painted black hair.

"Her name's Pansy," she told me with a smile. "Let's see if you have a nightgown in that bag of yours."

After she had helped me wash and change into my nightgown, she brought me supper—warm milk and bread and preserves. I sat in a rocking chair with a blanket around me. Pansy was in my arms, and I listened to Miss Tibbie talking but was too tired to take in what she was saying.

When Sarah came to the end of the entry, she saved it on the same disk as before, this time under the file name MYSTERY-2. Then she read it through again slowly. She read with such concentration that she could almost see the bedroom and the doll through the girl's eyes. She noticed that the Dewey House and Dewey Shopping Plaza shared the same name. But where did that get her?

While Sarah had been reading, a couple of kids had come into the store to sign up for the computer club. A boy and a girl. Sarah guessed they were around fourteen or fifteen. The boy was named Alan Dobson and the girl, Rachel Rose. Rachel was tall with bouncy dark hair. She looked around the store, commenting on just about everything. Sarah smiled eagerly, but the smile froze on her face when the girl looked right past her. She wondered if maybe she'd become invisible—like the ghost in the computer.

That was the first time Sarah had admitted, even to herself, that the computer store was haunted. Haunted by the ghost of a little girl with curly dark hair and a pointed chin. She explored the idea cautiously, carefully, as if she were running her tongue over a tooth that might hurt and bracing herself for the pain. But there was no stab of fear when she thought about the ghost in the computer. The feeling was closer to friendship and sympathy. Maybe because the ghost girl's father had said to that Mrs. Jardine that she was no trouble and was used to amusing herself—almost the same words her own dad had said to the apartment manager.

Sarah watched Alan and Rachel breeze out. As they left they told Mr. Pearce he'd see them on Saturday morning, for sure.

"Nice kids," Mr. Pearce said.

Sarah nodded noncommittally.

She leaned back in her chair and looked around the store at the molded plastic tables and the smooth lines of the computers and printers, the shelves of books with titles like *The Fundamentals of Basic Programming*, and the racks of disks and games. There was no way a ghost could be haunting the store! The only thing that even remotely suggested the supernatural was the rack of games with names like Wizardry and Zork. That must be the answer, Sarah told herself with a sigh of relief. Somehow a computer-game virus was caught up in the machine's random-access memory—or was it in its read-only memory?

Having satisfied herself with this new explanation, Sarah reached around to the back of her computer and switched it off. She watched the letters fade, but as the screen grew dark the strange reflection began to reappear. She could see it clearly now. Someone was staring back at her from the computer screen—a young girl with dark, anxious, pleading eyes.

4

Why?

The following morning Sarah stayed home. She started to write a letter to Tina, but the only thing she could think of to write about was the ghost, and she didn't know how to begin. She tried reading, but she couldn't concentrate. She finally threw the book aside and called her dad. She was supposed to let him know where she was going when she went out. But before she could tell him that she was going to the park, Mr. Pearce snapped, "After this, Sarah, would you please make sure to turn off your computer before you go home?"

"But I did!" Sarah answered.

"It was on this morning—in fact, it's still on."

"I know I turned it off," Sarah insisted.

Ordinarily it would be hard to be one hundred percent sure about something like that, but those dark, pleading eyes weren't something Sarah could easily forget.

Then she had another thought.

"What's on the screen, Dad?" she asked.

"Let's see . . . Oh, yes—'Where is the Dewey House?' "

" 'Where is the Dewey House?' " Sarah repeated. "That's all?"

Sarah had hoped there would be a softball game going on at the park, so that she could blend in with the spectators and at least pretend to be part of whatever was happening in Dixon Landing. She was growing very tired of always being on her own. But the park was deserted except for three little kids who were earnestly pushing the merry-go-round with no one riding on it. Sarah wasn't that desperate for company, so she cut across the park to Baker Street, deciding she'd go to the Big Apple after all. But when she reached Baker Street she had another thought. According to the story on the computer, the Dewey House was somewhere on Baker Street, near the edge of town. She set off to look for it. The only thing she had to go on was that it had a front porch. The sycamores and chestnut trees lining the street were so big that their branches met overhead, making Sarah feel as though she were walking through a green tunnel. Farther up the street the houses were mostly one story and didn't have porches. Then she came to the high dormitory buildings on the campus. She turned around and walked back down the other side of the street. She was back at the shopping plaza when it occurred to her that long ago the edge of town would have been only a few blocks from the river.

The first thing Sarah noticed when she went into the store was that the computer was still on. She slid into the blue and chrome chair in front of the monitor, pushing her hair back behind her ears, and stared at the words WHERE IS THE DEWEY HOUSE? It wasn't fair of the computer to throw questions at her when what she needed was answers. She punched in her question: WHY? Then she leaned back in her chair, waiting to see what would happen.

Afterward she had a hard time remembering exactly what did happen. One moment she was looking into the computer, seeing the ghost girl sitting in a small rocking chair, holding a doll. The next moment Sarah herself was rocking back and forth in her chair. When she looked down at her lap, she saw the doll's white china face staring up at her. Someone was talking to her, but she didn't want to listen to what he was saying. She rocked harder. Back and forth.

"Mr. and Mrs. Jardine and Tibbie want you to stay here with them," the voice was saying.

The voice came from somewhere over her head, but she didn't look up. In her line of vision she could see a pair of black boots and rather shiny black trousers. She continued to rock. Back and forth. Back and forth. She'd never felt this bad before—*never*—so filled with sadness that her whole body ached.

"Sam will be like a brother to you. Won't it be nice having a big brother?" the voice continued.

She didn't want a brother. Especially not Sam Jardine. Just yesterday morning he'd put a black beetle in her cup. Deliberately. He'd wanted to hear her scream. But she didn't. She'd scooped the beetle out of the cup and hidden it in her pocket till she could set it free outside. No, she didn't want that pesky Sam Jardine for a brother!

She only wanted her mother.

And that was what was hurting so much. Dear Mama was dead. Mama, who had been so full of music and laughter. How could Papa go right on with his life—traveling off to San Francisco with the Opera Company?

"It will only be for a short while," he told her. "We'll be well paid in San Francisco and I'll send the Jardines money for your keep."

She held Pansy tight, still refusing to look up. It had been a mistake to have been so little trouble here in the Dewey House. She should have fussed and screamed when she saw that beetle. The Jardines might not have agreed to keep her if she hadn't always been so quiet.

"It'll be better for you here with Miss Tibbie than forever moving from one hotel room to another," Papa's voice continued. "You'll go to school here, and then you can write me letters. When I come back I'll bring you a lovely new doll."

Mama had already taught her to read and write. And she knew she would hate going to school with a lot of other children.

She only said, "I don't need a doll. I've got Pansy." She choked back her tears.

But when it came time for Papa to leave, the tears spilled over. She clung to him and sobbed and begged him to take her along. He might have, but Clara Whitehorn was with him, and Clara didn't like children.

"I'll be back soon, *mon petit chou!*" Papa said, holding her tight. "I'll be back soon. Promise me you'll be waiting right here in this house when I come back!"

"I promise!" she sobbed. "I promise! I'll wait here for you forever."

Tears were streaming down her face so hard she couldn't see clearly. For a moment she thought Papa had walked back into the room, when she heard someone asking her what on earth was wrong.

"Sarah! What is it?" Mr. Pearce repeated.

His voice wasn't in the least like Papa's.

"Nothing, Dad!" Sarah answered, scrubbing her eyes with her fists.

Her dad and Ben and even a customer who'd just walked into the shop were all staring at her.

She couldn't begin to tell them about the terrible sadness of Mama dying and Papa going away and leaving her. She was left groping for a plausible reason for all those tears.

"I was reading this sad story . . ."

Her dad raised one eyebrow slightly.

"At least, I was remembering it. . . ." Sarah jumped up and pushed between her dad and Ben and headed for the storeroom behind the counter. She didn't bother to switch on the light. As she sank down on a carton of waste paper several white plastic pellets that had spilled out of a packing case swirled around her feet like leaves blowing on a sidewalk. She sat there for a long time and must have drifted off to sleep, because the phone ringing in the store brought her back to herself with a start. The sadness of Mama dying still clung to her mind like damp fog, though now it was more like remembering a dream.

Yet it was more vivid than a dream. The way Papa had talked. And the girl's promise to wait for him. So that was how the Dewey House fit into the picture! The ghost had answered her WHY? She had promised her father that she'd wait there until he came back from San Francisco. With a sudden flash of intuition Sarah also guessed what had happened to the Dewey House. It must have been pulled down to make way for the Dewey Shopping Plaza, leaving the poor ghost with nowhere to wait.

5

The Computer Club

On Friday evening Sarah's mom had a seminar until six o'clock, so the Pearces were eating dinner at Papa's Pizza. Sarah had wanted to go there because the name reminded her of the entries on the disk, but now, as she ate her way along a thread of melted cheese, she was wishing they'd had the pizza delivered. The kids at the next table were singing "Happy Birthday to You" at the top of their voices and—even though it was totally unreasonable—Sarah was feeling left out. She could tell they'd all known one another forever. Probably this time next year she'd still be going out for pizza with her parents. . . .

She turned her back on the party and asked her dad, "Have you any idea what was there before they built the shopping center?"

"Houses, I believe," Mr. Pearce answered. "The city council showed a lot of foresight in rezoning the site for stores. Too many times new shopping malls are built out in the suburbs and the downtown dies."

"Taking down a house isn't fair to the people who lived there," Sarah protested.

"The building was probably empty, Sarah. And even if it wasn't, they'd find somewhere else for the tenants to go."

Her mom added something about change being inevitable. Then she went on to say that Sarah shouldn't be spending all her time in the Big Apple. She should go over to the Aquatic Center or the park, so she could meet people before school started.

Sarah reached for another piece of pizza. She guessed her dad must have told her mom about her crying at the store.

"I know it isn't easy getting used to new surroundings, Sarah," her mom continued. "Especially when your dad and I are both so busy and you're alone a lot."

"Next you'll be turning me into a thesis study on a maladjusted only child!" Sarah growled.

"You really want to go down and stay with Tina, don't you?" her mom asked gently.

"No, I don't!"

"Maybe we could arrange something with Tina's family."

"No!"

Sarah was surprised at how strongly she felt. She didn't want to go back to Menlo Park. Not now. Not till she knew more about the people who had lived in the Dewey House. But how could she ever explain that to her parents? If her mom knew that she was worrying about a ghost, she'd end up being a thesis project for sure!

"Tomorrow's the computer club," her dad said. "You'll get to know a few kids that way."

"You've just finished telling me I shouldn't be spending so much time at the Big Apple," Sarah argued.

"Oh, Sarah! You know that wasn't what we meant!"

"I'm not really into computers," Sarah said.

"How can you say that after spending all week staring at one? Of course you'll be there!"

"Dad's counting on you," her mom chimed in.

"There's that nice boy, Jeff Cuff."

"I hear that at least two girls have signed up . . ."

"Rachel and Rose . . ."

They sounded as if they had rehearsed a script.

"That's the same girl," Sarah interrupted. She'd checked the list over carefully. There were two girls— Rachel Rose and Beth Cohen. Les Metzgar could be either a boy or a girl. The others were Alan Dobson, Tom Williams, Mitch Evanson, and Herb Halliday.

Then she had another thought. She had to be there—to keep an eye on her computer.

Les turned out to be a girl. A thin girl with glasses. She didn't look much older than Sarah, but she knew so much about computers that she could have been in high school. Even Herb Halliday, who was a junior, asked her advice. The other two girls were around fifteen. Sarah hovered in the background.

"Watch this!" Alan said, and everyone crowded in to see. His nobbly fingers raced over the keys. "I think I'll sell this program to Mr. Pearce! It would make a great ad. The computer draws an apple and the words 'Have a byte!' appear under it."

"It's a pun: *B-Y-T-E!*" Rachel Rose spelled out. Her voice oozed admiration.

Sarah went over to her usual computer and loaded Applewriter. With everyone bunched around Alan there were computers to spare. She wasn't interested in writing her own programs, and she was pretty sure that no one was going to include her in games like Zork. She might as well get on with her autobiography. Rachel's talking about puns had reminded her of the day she'd had a fight with April Kerr back in second grade. April had joined Sarah's class in January, so she was still quite new on Valentine's Day. Sarah's mom had bought her a box of assorted valentines— the kind with cute animals making bad puns. A lion saying, "I'm li-on in wait for you!" and a bee saying, "Honey, bee mine!" For April, Sarah had picked out a card with a chimpanzee saying, "I go ape over you!" How could she have known that April went bananas when people called her Ape? She'd burst into tears and had ripped up the valentine. Of course she'd been called Ape from that day on.

Sarah typed the heading SCHOOL and was leaning

back in her seat trying to recall the jokes on the other valentines when it happened again. Her story faded from the screen and another entry appeared in its place. It was also about school. Even though Sarah had no reason to think she knew the rules, she hadn't expected the ghost to reach out to her with the store so crowded. But when she began to read the new entry, she soon forgot there was anyone else around.

SCHOOL

There were good things and bad things about school, though it often seemed that the bad things far outnumbered the good. Mama had already taught me to read. I liked my reading book, even though I found it easy, and I could write on my slate more neatly than a lot of the older children.

The bad things mostly happened because of Sam Jardine. He teased me at home and he teased me at school. On the very first day of school, when we were setting off across the yard, he chanted in a singsong voice, "Turn around and close your eyes and you will get a big surprise." I didn't notice that his pet Angora goat was loose in the yard. Of course, the moment I turned my back the pesky goat butted me and I landed in a puddle of mud. I couldn't return to the house and face Mrs. Jardine, so I trudged on to school. It got me off to a bad start with my teacher, Miss Carruthers, who put cleanliness ahead of godliness.

Each morning before school started, Miss Carruthers used to look at our hands and nails to make sure that they were clean. Even though I scrubbed my hands before I left home, I could never walk to school without picking stones out of the gutter or feeling the sticky buds of the chestnut tree. One day I brought a baby bird to school in my pocket after Sam had knocked down its nest. Miss Carruthers might have forgiven me, except I'd brought worms in my other pocket to feed the poor bird.

Another problem was that I often mixed French and English words. Miss Carruthers never could understand that the French name sometimes had a better sound than the English. An *église* brings to mind a place to worship God, while a church sounds more like a cough or a sneeze. And surely *hirondelle* is a better name for a graceful bird than swallow!

I'd learned French from Papa. His father had been a French-Canadian voyageur. His mother was an Indian chief's daughter. Papa often told me the French names for things as we traveled up and down the river through the forest. Although he loved singing with the opera, I knew he was missing the animals and flowers of the woods while he was in

San Francisco. He'd surely come back to Oregon soon.

Sarah's fingers trembled as she hit Save and transferred the story to the disk. Then she cleared the screen. As the words faded she saw the face again, the large eyes, the pointed chin and curly hair. Then the words HELP ME FIND THE DEWEY HOUSE appeared.

"How did you make it do that?"

Sarah jumped nervously at the sound of a voice behind her. Jeff Cuff was frowning at the screen.

"I don't do it—it just happens."

"That stuff you wrote . . . about Sam Jardine and school—"

"You had no right to read that!"

"I thought the idea of this club was for us to learn from each other. I wish you'd show me how you made that face flicker and then fade out."

"I didn't do it," Sarah said, though this time she didn't sound quite so indignant. She desperately wanted to tell someone about the strange way the computer was acting. She just wasn't sure that Jeff Cuff was the right person.

"How do you know about Sam Jardine, anyway?" he asked.

"About Sam Jardine?"

"Yeah—that he had a pet goat. I've seen a picture of it."

"Where did you see it?"

Jeff didn't answer.

His blue-eyed stare was making Sarah feel uneasy, yet there was something disturbingly familiar about him. Perhaps that was what made her whisper, "I think . . . I think there's a ghost in the computer."

"I suppose next you'll say it's Pascale."

This was not the answer Sarah had expected.

"Pascal? The computer language?" she asked.

"Very funny," Jeff said. He dragged a chair over and sat down next to Sarah. "Pascale, the girl! Everybody knows Pascale! You must have heard about the ghost who haunted the Dewey House."

Sarah shook her head.

"My little sister once saw her." Then Jeff's voice took on what was meant to be a sinister tone. "It was a dark and stormy night, and we were on our way home from the library when Molly—that's my sister—saw Pascale looking out an upstairs window. A sad, white face . . ."

"When was this?"

"A couple of years ago, before the house was moved."

"Moved?" Sarah said. The word came out so loud that some of the other kids looked across at her and Jeff. "You mean to say they didn't just tear it down?"

"The city auctioned it off, and then it had to be moved so that they could build the shopping center here," Jeff explained.

"So the house is still standing somewhere?" Sarah asked, her voice rising with excitement.

"Of course," Jeff answered. "At the end of Pioneer Lane. It was only moved last summer. It was the biggest thing that's happened in Dixon Landing in years. People lined the streets—though you'd hardly think that watching a truck drive along Second Street at a top speed of a block an hour would be a spectator sport! But you must have heard of the Dewey House. Or else how could you have written about the people who lived in it?"

"I told you, I didn't write it. It came on the computer by itself. There's more . . . if you'd like to see it."

Jeff hunched over the screen and read through each of the entries on the disk.

"You say you didn't write any of this?" he asked when he'd finished.

"I did write some of it," Sarah admitted. "That part about her papa leaving her. That wasn't on the screen. It was more like I was there . . . in her thoughts."

As soon as she said it, she knew she was pushing Jeff too far. Expecting him to believe something as weird as that.

"Or maybe I dreamed that part," she added quickly. "But the rest really was on the computer."

Jeff loaded the second entry and read it through again. Sarah watched him, trying to guess from his expression what he was thinking.

"So what do you make of it?" she asked when he reached the end.

"You sure know how to tell a good story," Jeff said, pushing back his chair.

The other kids were gathering up their things and getting ready to leave.

"It's not a story—it's real!" Sarah insisted.

A crackling sound, like static, came from somewhere behind the computer and the words HELP ME FIND MY WAY HOME flashed across the screen.

"You're pretty good at programming, too," Jeff added.

Without another word he turned and walked out of the store.

6

Baby-sitting Molly

On Monday morning the phone rang while the Pearces were eating breakfast.

"It's for you, Sarah!" Mrs. Pearce said.

"For me?" Sarah asked in surprise. The phone was never for her these days.

She almost dropped the receiver when the caller identified herself as Mrs. Cuff. What on earth could Jeff's mother want? Sarah missed the first part of what Mrs. Cuff was saying because she was so busy running over the possibilities in her mind.

"Because Debbie, my regular sitter, just called in sick. Jeff has a Parks and Rec soccer game, and I have to go to work—I'm a dietician at the hospital. I'm due there in half an hour. Jeff said I should try you—that you're new in town and spend a lot of time at your dad's store. Molly won't give you any trouble"

"I'll ask my mom," Sarah said, breaking into the flow of words.

Covering the receiver with her hand, Sarah said, "Mrs. Cuff wants me to baby-sit—right now."

"For how many children?"

"One, I think—a girl—Molly."

Sarah's parents held a quick conference. The only time Sarah had baby-sat was for Tina's brothers, and Tina had always been there too. Mr. Pearce said that Jeff was a nice, steady boy. Her mom said she could drop Sarah off at the Cuffs' house on her way to Dixon College. That way she could meet Mrs. Cuff. Sarah, meantime, was thinking about Jeff saying that his little sister had once seen Pascale. She'd like to hear what Molly had to say about it.

The Cuffs' front yard had a well-used look. A bright pink scooter lay abandoned on the grass and a half-constructed skateboard ramp occupied the driveway. Mrs. Cuff was waiting at the door, looking like a woman in a soap commercial in her gleaming uniform. Or maybe a toothpaste commercial. She had a very white smile. She exchanged a few words with Mrs. Pearce, then ushered Sarah in and gave her a crash course on mothering, homemaking, and first aid, with Molly trailing behind them.

Sarah liked the Cuffs' house immediately. The furniture was worn and comfortable. Books and magazines were stacked on the coffee table. A half-finished mug of coffee sat next to a vase of cosmos that had shed a ring of golden pollen and dropped a few petals on the dusty surface. Real flowers, even wilted ones, were a lot better than blue and yellow pansies made of china.

"Ed's out in the field this week," Mrs. Cuff said as she pinned her work phone number for Sarah on the bulletin board beside the phone.

Sarah formed a mental picture of a horse, but when Mrs. Cuff added that these crises always happened when Ed was away, Sarah decided Ed must be Jeff and Molly's dad.

"Jeff should be home before I am," Mrs. Cuff continued. "He'll help you baby-sit."

Sarah wasn't sure that this was good news. She was still wondering what had prompted Jeff to tell his mom to call her.

"Not that you'll need help," Mrs. Cuff added as she went out the door. "You'll find that Molly's a quiet little girl."

Looking down at Molly's serious face and the tilt of her chin, Sarah thought that obstinate might be a better word. However, Molly turned out to be easy to look after. She was an unusually scheduled child. From eight thirty till nine she watched *Mister Rogers' Neighborhood* and *Sesame Street* from nine till ten. Then it was time to feed the guinea pigs, Alpha and Omega. Maybe having a mom who was a dietitian made Molly take food seriously. She gave them their ration of pellets with a side order of granola and raisins and fresh dandelion leaves. It took forever, and while they ate she told them the highlights from *Sesame Street*.

"Couldn't they just have watched it for themselves?" Sarah asked.

"They did!" Molly answered. "But they want to hear it again."

Next she fetched her weather chart. Sarah sat down at the kitchen table across from Molly and watched the little girl carefully cut out a yellow sun and paste it in the right square.

"We did this every day last year in first grade."

"Jeff told me that you once saw a ghost in the Dewey House," Sarah said quietly. "What was she like?"

Molly looked up from her weather chart through her wispy hair with a wary expression in her eyes.

"Jeff said I'm not supposed to talk about it," Molly whispered.

"Why not?" Sarah asked.

"Because he wants to be here, too, when you tell us some more Pascale stories," Molly explained. "That's why he asked Mom to get you to baby-sit."

"He wasn't all that interested in Pascale on Saturday," Sarah snapped. "Anyway, he's heard everything there is to hear."

"I wish it would lightning," Molly said, frowning. "I have a lot of spare lightning."

"Was there lightning that night you saw Pascale?" Sarah asked.

Molly shook her head. "No, but the wind was blowing."

"So there was a bad windstorm?" Sarah prompted, hoping to lead Molly on.

"We'd been at the library," Molly said. "I dropped one of my books on the way to the car, and the wind went whipping through the pages, like it was reading really fast." She giggled.

Sarah smiled encouragingly.

"The trees in front of the old Dewey House were creaking and moaning." Molly was beginning to enjoy herself. "I looked up at their branches, clawing the paint off the walls . . . and that's when I saw her! She was at the bedroom window. Crying because she—"

At that moment Jeff came bursting through the back door, kicking off his shoes and sliding across the kitchen floor all in one motion. He slammed to a stop next to Molly.

"Are you talking about Pascale?" he asked, glaring down at his little sister. His hair was sticking up even more than usual and he had grass stains all over his shirt.

"It's a free country," Sarah put in. "We can talk about whatever we choose."

"I've got some questions I wanted to ask you about your ghost," Jeff said. "And I didn't want you finding out about our family from Molly before I got here."

"About *your* family?" Sarah repeated. "What do they have to do with anything?"

"The Dewey House was built by someone in our family," Jeff said. "I asked Mom about it last night. She might not have it all straight, but she'd heard of some of those people you wrote about—like Alfred and Maud."

"She knows about the Jardines!" Sarah said. She was so excited that she let the words "that you wrote about" slide right past her. "That could really help us find out what's going on. How are you related to them?"

"Mom figures my great-great-great-grandfather built the Dewey House. At least we think it's three greats. His name was Daniel Dewey. Sam Jardine—the boy you wrote about—was my great-grandfather."

"Yeah . . . I think I see a family likeness," Sarah said slowly. "Around the eyes . . . and the way your hair always sticks up in front. And if he was alive now, I bet he'd have braces."

"Very funny!" Jeff said. "Next you'll be saying you've seen him hanging out in the computer store too!"

Sarah didn't answer. The way she could see Sam Jardine so clearly in her mind frightened her a little. As if she'd actually known him. Pascale's thoughts and hers had been so close that Sarah knew exactly how Sam Jardine had looked that morning at breakfast all those years ago, when he waited for Pascale to discover the beetle in her cup.

"What's the matter?" Jeff asked. "You really are scared, aren't you?"

"I just wish I knew what's going on," Sarah said. Her voice shook as she added, "You've got to believe me, Jeff! I'm not leading you on! How could I have made that story up, if Sam Jardine is a real person?"

"Maybe you read about the Jardines in the library," Jeff said.

"I did not!" Sarah said. She jumped to her feet and added, "If you're not going to believe me, then I don't want to talk about it. You can look after Molly till your mom comes home. You can tell her you didn't like Molly associating with a liar!"

"You can't go!" Molly wailed. "Jeff hasn't told you yet how he thinks Pascale ended up in your dad's store."

Sarah raised her eyebrows. Perhaps Jeff didn't doubt her as much as he'd made out. She sat down again, waiting for him to begin.

"Molly was wondering why Pascale didn't just move with the house, and that got me wondering, too," Jeff said. "But suppose she only materializes every now and then—when there's someone on this side that she can reach. She might not have been there when they moved the house. Then she comes back and a computer store is where the house should be. Now she wants to get back to the house, because she promised her dad she'd be waiting for him there. But she can't get back to it unless someone calls her."

"Who lives in the house now?" Sarah asked.

"Old Thelma Gibson. She bought it when the city auctioned it off last year. Even though she got it for a few thousand dollars, people thought she was crazy, saddling herself with that big house at her age."

"Why did she want it?" Sarah asked.

"She was just buying back what she said was rightfully hers," Jeff explained. "Thelma Gibson is Tibbie Dewey's youngest daughter. Daniel Dewey—he's the guy who is my three-greats grandfather—left the Dewey House to his two daughters, Maud and Tibbie. When Maud married Alfred Jardine, Tibbie stayed on in the house with them. Then Tibbie fell in love with some guy that Alfred didn't like. So she ran off with him, and Alfred tried to stop her by blowing up the sternwheeler they were on. . . ."

Sarah couldn't quite follow the genealogy, but she did get the meaning of Jeff's last statement.

"Alfred tried to murder poor Tibbie?" she shrieked.

"That's what people said—though nothing was ever proved. There was never a trial because Alfred died of a heart attack a short while after. The house went to Sam Jardine, and then to his son Danny, and Tibbie got nothing. Not that there was much to get. The Jardines' hardware business went downhill on account of all the gossip and scandal."

"Danny must be your grandfather," Sarah said, counting off the generations on her fingers.

Jeff shook his head.

"He's my great-uncle. His sister Emily was my grandmother. She moved to California before my dad was born, and he grew up there. When we came back here a few years ago, the Jardines were all dead and the Dewey House had been taken over by the city for back taxes. Thelma Gibson was the only one left. She wouldn't have anything to do with us because we were from the Jardine side. But Dad didn't lose much sleep over that!"

"What about Pascale? What happened to her?" Sarah asked.

"No one really knows," Jeff said. "Maybe she died in the explosion—though I don't think anyone was killed. Or she could have run away to San Francisco to look for her dad."

"She wouldn't have done that," Sarah said firmly. "Not after promising to wait for him. She didn't leave the Dewey House voluntarily."

"I wonder how we could find out what happened to her," Jeff said.

Sarah liked hearing him say "we," as if he was coming around to believing in the ghost. Sometimes she had to remind herself that only a week ago she wouldn't have believed it either.

"Yeah, what we need to do is find out everything we can about Pascale," Jeff continued. "We can take turns watching the computer for messages. Maybe we could sneak into the store at night. That would be the best time for getting messages. On a dark, stormy night with a new moon."

Sarah sighed. Jeff didn't really believe in Pascale after all. Not properly, or he wouldn't be thinking up schemes like that. She was almost relieved to hear Mrs. Cuff's cheery voice asking, "Where is everyone?"

Molly hurled herself into her mother's arms.

"We've been talking about Pascale," she said. "Sarah's seen her too!"

Mrs. Cuff laughed and gave Molly a hug. "Poor Pascale! I thought she would have been laid to rest when old Thelma Gibson gave the Dewey House a fresh coat of paint and knocked down all the cobwebs."

"She lives in the Big Apple now," Molly said.

"Speaking of apples, who wants lunch?" Mrs. Cuff asked with a friendly chuckle.

As well as apples, Mrs. Cuff served grated carrot, raisin, and honey sandwiches on whole-grain bread—the kind with husks in it—and plain yogurt. Sarah had the passing thought that having a dietician for a mother would be worse than having a mother studying child psychology. But when Mrs. Cuff asked if she'd like to fill in for Debbie some other time, Sarah was more than willing. The morning hadn't gone too badly after all.

7

Earthquake!

Mrs. Cuff dropped Sarah off at the Big Apple.

"How did it go?" her dad asked when she walked into the store.

"Fine, Dad! Molly was no trouble at all. She's a nice little kid."

"How about typing up some handouts for next Saturday's computer club?"

"Handouts!" Sarah exclaimed. "You can't give them handouts, Dad. This isn't school!"

"A couple of kids need more BASIC for the programs they're writing," her dad answered, smiling. "They *asked* me for this, Sarah. And I promise there'll be no quizzes or grades!"

Sarah took the sheets and sat down at the computer. She was pretty sure Pascale wasn't around, although she couldn't have explained exactly how she knew. It was just that there was a different feeling in the store—or in Sarah—when Pascale was there. A sort of anticipating feeling, like she sometimes had when she woke in the morning, knowing something big was going to happen that day, but not yet awake enough to know what it was. Not even awake enough to be sure if it was something good or bad.

While Sarah was typing, she thought about Pascale. She had a plan—of sorts—and was wondering if it would work. Jeff had told her the way to the Dewey House and it sounded quite straightforward. North on Second to the edge of town. Pioneer Lane was the first road to the right. The house was at the end of Pioneer Lane on the Willamette River. She was going to leave the directions on the computer, so Pascale could go there by herself. Though she wasn't sure she was ready to let Pascale leave. There was still so much she wanted to find out. She didn't even know exactly when Pascale had lived in the Dewey House.

And there was Jeff to think about. He'd be disappointed if there were no more entries on the computer.

Sarah ran off the first three pages of the handout, then typed in the heading of a new section—apparently about identifying problems in a program. It was called LOOKING FOR BUGS. But as the words appeared on the screen Sarah felt that almost familiar whisper of coldness. She was scarcely surprised when the computer took over and began an entry of its own.

Even though the beetles and caterpillars and snails I brought to school in my pockets were not well received, Miss Carruthers did encourage us to study nature. One April morning she told us how tadpoles turn into frogs, and she asked if someone could bring a jar of frog spawn to school so that we could watch the tadpoles grow. Always eager to make her like me better, I made up my mind I'd be the one to bring the frog's eggs. At lunchtime I raced home and found a jar. Carefully I tied a piece of string around its neck and made a loop for the handle. Then I set off for the boggy field west of town, where the frogs croaked so loudly in the spring that you could hear them all over Dixon Landing.

When I reached the bog, I took off my boots and stockings and squished through the mud. I had just filled the jar with spawn when I heard the distant peal of the school bell. It was time for afternoon classes to begin. How could the lunch hour have gone by so fast when other days it was so long? Clutching my boots in one hand, the jar swinging in the other, slopping muddy water over my dress, I raced toward the school. Somewhere along the way I tripped. The jar shattered and I didn't even spare a thought for the poor eggs that would never turn into frogs. I picked myself up and ran on. Miss Carruthers put punctuality ahead of cleanliness.

She didn't understand my breathless explanation. And I didn't have the jar of frog spawn to prove my story. She frowned at my dirty feet and muddy dress and made me stand in the corner. It was while I was standing there that someone came rushing in to say that there had been a great earthquake in San Francisco. I trembled, thinking of my papa.

Poor Pascale! So that was why Papa never returned. He must have been hurt—or killed—in the big San Francisco earthquake. After the October 'quake Sarah had seen pictures on TV of the earlier one. San Francisco had burned for three days and hundreds of people had died. It had been far worse than the recent earthquake—and that was bad enough. She tried to remember when the first one had happened. Nineteen hundred and six, she thought. April 1906.

"Are you finished with the handouts?" Mr. Pearce asked, jerking Sarah back to the present.

"Not yet," she admitted. "Would it be okay if I did the rest later?"

She had other things to think about now.

"There's no real hurry," her dad answered. "We don't need them till Saturday."

Sarah saved the new entry as MYSTERY-4 on Pascale's disk and then called Jeff at home.

"It fits," he said when he heard about the earthquake. "The snapshot I told you about—of Sam Jardine and his goat—was taken at a Fourth of July parade in 1906. That would be later the same year. I went through a bunch of old pictures last night and found it."

"Does Sam look like you?" Sarah asked.

"No way!" Jeff laughed. "Though you can't really make out his face. He's sitting in a little cart with a flat straw hat on his head. I think the picture was taken in front of the Occidental Hotel on Second Street."

"Maybe you could bring it down here tomorrow and I could show you this latest entry."

"I have soccer in the morning," Jeff said. "But I might drop by in the afternoon."

He didn't sound exactly eager. Sarah felt rebuffed.

The next morning, however, Jeff did show up. He came straight from practice, so he didn't bring the picture.

"Anything new?" he asked, peering over Sarah's shoulder at the screen.

"Just the entry I told you about," Sarah said. "But Pascale's around this morning. She did something to the electricity and Dad lost a customer."

"How do you mean 'lost a customer'?" Jeff asked, wide-eyed.

"Dad was demonstrating a program to this guy.

When all the numbers vanished off the screen, he said he wanted something reliable and walked out of the store."

"Oh, I imagined something worse . . ."

"Having a ghost mess up the computers isn't exactly good for business."

"I've been thinking about how we could get her out of here," Jeff said, sitting down. "I once read this book where they trapped ghosts in bottles. It's called exorcising them."

"If we had her in a bottle, we could take her to the Dewey House and leave her there," Sarah said.

"Yeah, we could jog over and exercise while we were exorcising!" Jeff laughed.

Sarah scowled. She wished Jeff would take Pascale seriously. This wasn't some sort of computer game they were making up between them.

"How do we get her into the bottle?" Sarah asked.

"That's the tricky part. You need a circle of candles—and of course it has to be done in the dark. I'll look up the details, though we probably have to modify them for a computer ghost. Maybe it would help if I could see her in action. Start a new entry and see if she takes over."

"What'll I write about?" Sarah asked. Even though she wanted Jeff's help, she resented the way he was suddenly such an authority on ghosts. Pascale may have lived in his ancestors' house, but it was Sarah she'd reached out to.

"Try pioneer women," Jeff suggested.

"I bet Pascale didn't call herself a pioneer woman," Sarah scoffed.

"How about earthquakes, then? That's what she was writing about at the end of the last entry. You could tell her about the October earthquake. You must have felt it in Menlo Park."

"We sure did," Sarah said. "Tina and I were leaving the library when everything went crazy. She threw down her books and started running, but I stayed right next to the building even though I knew that wasn't the best place to be. My legs refused to go where my brain told them. When the earthquake finally quit there was dust everywhere—and the noise! The shaking had set off all the fire and burglar alarms."

"I wish I'd been there," Jeff said enviously. "It must have been exciting."

"It was awful!" Sarah told him. "Dad was at the World Series and it was hours before we knew he was safe. Then the aftershocks went on for days."

Sarah began to type. As she did so the lights in the store flickered and Mr. Pearce swore because something had gone wrong with his computer again.

"I'm going to have to see the contractors about the wiring in this building," he said to Ben. "These power surges we get all the time could do no end of damage."

Neither Jeff nor Sarah glanced in his direction. Their

eyes were riveted on the story unfolding in front of them on the computer.

THE EARTHQUAKE

At first, when no word came from Papa, I was sure that he was making his way back to Dixon Landing. I told myself that the big fire after the earthquake would have burned up all the post offices, so he couldn't mail a letter. I knew that he would come back because he'd made me promise to wait for him. But days turned into weeks, weeks into months, and still he didn't appear. Nor was there any letter. When the money didn't come for my room and board, Maud Jardine told me I would have to earn my keep. So that was the end of my schooling.

When Maud said Papa must be dead, I refused to listen. I ran out of the kitchen and up to my bedroom. The room was stifling hot, so I propped the window open with a heavy book. Then I sat in the chair in the corner, staring at the pink and red roses on the wallpaper, and rocked Pansy. Papa had told me to wait for him. I knew he'd come. Someone downstairs was calling me, but I didn't answer.

"Where is that dratted girl? Always skulking off

somewhere when there's work to do." The voice was drawing closer and sounded slightly breathless. Maud was on her way upstairs to look for me.

I slid under the bed. The patchwork counterpane didn't quite reach the floor, so I wriggled farther under, bumping the china chamber pot. A moment later Maud came into the room. I squinted along the floor at her black leather shoes with pointed toes and the hem of her blue dress.

"What's that book doing there?" she muttered to herself. "Why, it's the Bible! What blasphemy!"

Hardly daring to breathe, I listened to the staccato sound of her shoes on the bare floor as she stomped across the room. She raised the window, then closed it firmly. The feet retreated and the door slammed shut.

I waited quite a long time before venturing out. My first thought was the window. I hate the trapped feeling of being in a room with the window closed. Tibbie had asked Alfred to fix the sash cord weeks ago, but he still hadn't done anything about it. I looked around for the big book, but Maud had taken it with her. There must be something else I could use to hold the window open. I grinned to myself. The chamber pot under the bed!

It wasn't easy to lift the heavy window sash with one hand while maneuvering the pot into place with the other. I was so intent on what I was doing that I didn't notice the man walking down the street until he was quite close to our house. For a moment I felt a glorious surge of happiness. . . . Papa had come for me . . . but the man walked past the house without even giving it a glance. My excitement turned to despair. It wasn't Papa after all. The chamber pot rolled forward out of my grasp and smashed into a thousand pieces when it hit the ground. Oh, dear, what was Maud going to say about that?

Sarah punched Save, transferring the words on the screen to the disk that held the rest of Pascale's story. Then in silence she and Jeff read the entry all the way through again.

"Now that you've seen it happen, you can't not believe in Pascale!" Sarah told Jeff, smiling happily. She felt like a parent whose small child had done something clever when company was present.

But Jeff was frowning. "You could have written that entry ahead of time and had it ready," he said.

"You told me to write 'Earthquake.' . . . You saw me do it!"

"That's exactly the point! That story doesn't have that much to do with earthquakes. You could have had it ready and just waited till I suggested something that vaguely tied in to what you'd already written."

"But Jeff, you were watching all the time! You saw it come on the screen by itself."

"Maybe you have a remote control," Jeff argued.

"I do not have a remote control!" Sarah shouted angrily. She was afraid she was going to cry. Jeff had wanted to see it happen—and it had. And now he was acting more skeptical than when he first walked into the store.

"Sounds as if someone needs a little *self*-control over there," Mr. Pearce said, and chuckled. He was glad to see that Sarah had a friend.

"I guess I'd better be going," Jeff said, getting to his feet.

"You can't leave, Jeff!" Sarah begged. "Not just when we've got some new evidence."

"Mom told me to come straight home."

"Oh, go ahead, then!"

Sarah was tempted to tell Jeff not to bother coming back ever, but she couldn't bear the thought of dealing with Pascale all by herself. She stared at the screen, the words "remote control" and "self-control" echoing through her mind. That's what it was like. Remote control. Pascale wanted to use her to somehow get back to the Dewey House . . . and she wanted to help the little girl. So why did she feel so shaken?

Maybe she should tell Pascale right now how to find the Dewey House down by the river. Without wasting any more time thinking about it, she began to type the directions into the computer: TO GET TO THE DEWEY HOUSE, GO DOWN TO THE OCCIDENTAL HOTEL AND TURN LEFT ON SECOND STREET. . . .

The store was so still that Sarah didn't think Pascale was around. She'd leave the computer on till she was sure the message had been received. All night, if necessary.

8

The Ghost's Story

On Wednesday morning Mr. Pearce didn't try to hide his exasperation when he saw that Sarah's computer had been left on once again. He went striding across the store with Sarah at his heels. She could see that the whole screen was filled with words. Her message had been changed. She just hoped that Pascale had read the directions first.

"What's all this about, anyway?" Mr. Pearce asked, leaning forward to read the entry. "The Dewey House—I wish it would stay . . ."

The monitor went dark.

"Now what? Have you been having problems with this computer, Sarah?"

Sarah shook her head. Her problems weren't with the computer.

"I'll have to get Ben to take a look at it when he comes in," her dad said. "He'll know what's going on—there's not much he can't figure out."

Sarah was pretty sure that even Ben wouldn't know

how to deal with a haunted keyboard, but she kept the thought to herself.

At that moment a woman in a rainbow-striped dress came sailing into the store. Sarah thought she looked like a walking ad for an Apple, but she turned out to be a weaver. She wanted to know about designing weaving patterns on a Macintosh, which led to exactly the sort of discussion Sarah's dad loved. Confident that he'd be busy for a while, Sarah sat down at the computer and typed THE DEWEY HOUSE.

Just as she had hoped, Pascale completed the entry. It had nothing to do with the directions Sarah had given, but seemed to be a description of the house after the Jardines no longer lived there.

I wish it would stay the same. One time when I came back, I hardly recognized the room I'd always looked on as my own. The flowered wallpaper was gone, and the bed with the patchwork quilt, and the little chair where I'd rocked away the hours waiting for Papa. The room had only the sparsest of furnishings—a narrow bed, a battered desk and chair, and a few wooden apple boxes filled with books. The other rooms were different, too. Some of the bigger ones had been divided into two—or even three—small rooms. The sofa in the living room was covered by a blanket to hide the threadbare upholstery. At all hours of the day people sprawled on it watching pictures on what

I soon learned was a television set. They crowded close to it, the way we used to crowd around the fire on a winter evening, but it did not seem so companionable. They all listened to the box instead of to one another.

The house was very noisy, echoing with the loud voices of young college students and radios and record players blaring from every room. The only improvement those people made was that they put a machine in the basement that washed clothes all by itself. I liked to sit down there in the dim light, watching the clothes go around and around in the sudsy water. My thoughts often drifted back to the old days. Maud's sharp-voiced scoldings when I let soapy water splash on the floor. The hard work of forcing the thick sheets through the old wringer and hanging the blankets on the clothesline, only to have to run out and fetch them in because it was raining. Many's the slap I got for letting the washing trail in the dirt. But I was only nine years old, and small for my age, so how could I help it? Ah, yes, this laundry machine was a great invention! All the same, I was so lonely that I found myself missing even Maud.

I used to talk to the students, but they didn't seem to hear me. They didn't see me, either. Though I never could have been friends with them the way I was with Sam Jardine. At first it had bothered me to watch Sam grow old while I remained forever young, but he told me he was glad to have my company. The two of us used to sit on the swing on the front porch and watch the world go by. And on winter evenings we'd sit by the fire and play cribbage. Sometimes he even let me win, which he'd never have done when I first knew him.

But there was one time when those students did see me. They often gave parties on weekends. On this occasion they'd been drinking too much and the party had turned wild. I was sitting on the window sill watching them, thinking how stupid they all were, when a man called James pointed me out to the others. They all made fun of him. But when I walked across the room and out into the hall, an uneasy silence fell. It was clear the rest of them could see me too. James swore never to touch another drop of alcohol; the others finished off the bottle fast.

Soon after that, the students moved away.

I liked the next people. They were quieter, gentler, than the students had been. Some of them had trouble hearing and speaking, and others had trouble seeing, yet I think most of them knew I was there. They didn't sleep in the house but came there every day to work. They made baskets and leather billfolds, and around Christmastime they made wreaths and other decorations. I grew very fond of a man named Clyde. I used to hold the evergreens for him while he twisted them together. The needles couldn't prick my fingers. Clyde was so proud when he made the most wreaths.

They hung the finished wreaths on the walls and displayed the decorations on shelves so that people could buy them. The house didn't seem so bare and empty now with cluttered tables and decorations and happy voices. A group of children came in one afternoon and sang carols. I sang along with them, and it was like Christmases long ago.

But one day some people came to look at the house, and they decided it wasn't safe. They said the wiring was too old. I heard the ones who were in charge of the house talking about it among themselves. When the fire marshal came to inspect the wiring, I did my best to scare him away by making the wires crackle and the lights flicker. I have this way with electricity. But I didn't save the house for my friends.

After they moved out, the house felt sad and empty. I'd promised to wait for Papa, but it was hard for me to stay there on my own. I wandered through the echoing rooms, singing the songs Papa once sang. Sometimes I stood at the window. Occasionally I would see someone walking along Fifth Street late at night and think that at last the long wait was over. But it was never Papa. And if the late-night walker happened to glance up at my window, he seldom answered my friendly salute. Instead he usually turned and ran.

This was followed by a time of terrible noise and confusion. Almost as if they were pulling the house down all around me and then putting it back together again. Perhaps that's what happened, because when I came back one day I found that everything had changed again. The Dewey House, with its porches and gables, was no longer there. Instead I was in a room where people typed whatever was in their minds and their thoughts appeared on black mirrors. Such uninteresting thoughts they had! Long lists of numbers and prices.

And then one day a girl with brown hair and dimples when she smiled . . .

Sarah searched the screen, but there was nothing more. A whisper of cold air touched the back of her neck and she shivered. In this entry Pascale was no longer a little girl. She was a ghost. Yet there was no clue as to what had happened to turn her into a ghost. Sarah read the entry again. The phrase "when I came back" implied Pascale wasn't always around. Where did she go between times? Out of habit Sarah saved the words on the screen. As she listened to the whirr of the disk drive she wondered if Pascale had read the directions. And if she had, then why was she still here? What else did she want Sarah to do for her?

Sarah looked at her dad, thinking that maybe she should try to tell him about the ghost after all, but he was still deep in conversation with the woman in the striped dress. Sarah watched them for a few minutes, wondering how close he was to making a sale. She hoped Pascale wouldn't do anything to mess it up.

A stutter of static drew her attention back to her own computer. She could see the woman's dress reflected in the screen, but the stripes seemed to be turning into flowers. Pink and red roses intertwined. Looking closer, she recognized the wallpaper in Pascale's room.

This time she tried to struggle against it. But Pascale was too strong for her. The computer store and Sarah slipped away and there was only Pascale. Pascale lying in bed under the patchwork quilt, looking at the roses on the wallpaper.

9

Jeff's Idea

When Sarah came back to herself—for that's how it seemed—she spent the rest of the morning watching the door for Jeff and watching the computer for Pascale. She was hoping Jeff would show up and Pascale wouldn't. She wished she hadn't been so touchy yesterday when Jeff accused her of having a remote control. After all, a haunted computer was too much to expect anyone to believe in. And what had happened this time was even weirder. So weird that she didn't want to think about it.

The hour hand crawled past eleven and on toward noon.

By lunchtime Sarah was worn out by watching and waiting. She decided she had to do something. Pascale's latest entry—the one about the Dewey House after it was rented out—provided an excuse for dropping by Jeff's house.

Jeff was surprisingly happy to see her, probably because he was baby-sitting Molly while their mom was shopping. Molly was equally happy. She dragged Sarah inside.

"What's new?" Jeff asked.

"Pascale left another message," Sarah answered. "I have a printout of it right here."

"Read it out loud," Molly demanded.

"Maybe you should read it to yourself, Jeff," Sarah said quietly. "It could scare Molly. It's about Pascale in the Dewey House when she was a ghost."

"Go ahead!" Jeff answered. "You don't need to worry about Molly. She doesn't scare easy! All she said the night she saw Pascale looking out the Dewey House window was 'Poor little ghost!' "

After Sarah finished reading, they were silent for a few moments. Then Jeff said, "It's weird the way everything ties in. I remember Dad saying that the house was rented out to college kids when the city first took it over. Then it was used as a work center for the handicapped."

"It ties in because that's the way it was," Sarah said. She tried to keep her voice friendly. She needed someone on her side—after yesterday. "I wish you'd believe me."

"I do believe you . . . I do . . . but it's more the way you believe in a movie while you're actually watching it, but afterward . . . when you get back home . . ."

"This isn't a movie, Jeff," Sarah said earnestly. "Something happened this morning that really scared me. I got dragged into Pascale's life again and it was as if I really was in her bedroom. Dad was talking to a customer and when I came back, he asked me where I'd been."

"Where *had* you been?" Jeff asked.

"I told you—I was in Pascale's bedroom. It was like a dream. Except that if it was just a dream, I'd have been sitting in front of the computer, asleep. But Dad thought I'd gone off somewhere."

"Did he see you leave?"

"I don't think so. He just noticed I wasn't at the computer."

"What was the dream—or whatever it was—about?"

"It started with a pattern of flowers on the screen. But when I looked closer, I realized that they were the roses on the wallpaper in Pascale's room. Pink and red roses intertwined."

"There isn't a color monitor on that set," Jeff pointed out.

"The roses weren't on the monitor—I was right there in Pascale's room, lying in her bed under the patchwork quilt. I didn't want to get out of bed because the room was cold. So I got dressed under the covers."

"In your clothes or hers?" Jeff asked.

"Hers," Sarah said, stifling a giggle. Jeff's teasing grin brought the spookiness back down to a level she could handle. "Cotton bloomers with a button instead of elastic and a wool undershirt, if you must know everything! Then when I heard someone coming, I jumped out of bed and pulled on these scratchy wool stockings and a long gray dress. While I was brushing my hair in front of the mirror, I remember feeling surprised at how I looked. The dark, curly hair and the shape of my face. As I was reaching for a white apron hanging on its peg behind the door I remembered it was washday. I'd have to wear the big stiff apron Maud had made out of heavy oilcloth instead. I hated washdays—the way they smelled of wet wool and lye soap and that nasty oilcloth apron!

"Down in the kitchen I raked the ashes out of the stove and carried them outside. Then Maud told me to light the fire under the boiler. Maud was wearing her best blue silk, so it didn't look as if she was going to help with the washing. Alfred was dressed up, too. And Sam."

"Did Sam help with lighting the fire?" Jeff asked.

Sarah shook her head. "No, but he did help fill the boiler with water. Though I ended up carrying more buckets of water than he did. I kept count. Then I followed Maud upstairs to strip the beds. Maud said Tibbie and I had to wash the blankets, too, because it was a good drying day."

"Then what?"

"Nothing—that was all," Sarah answered. "Someone walked into the store and I was back in my own time."

"That's not much of a story," Jeff complained. "Not that much happened."

"It's like I was caught up in something Pascale was remembering," Sarah said. "People think in snatches—not in stories. But what really scares me is Dad asking me where I'd been. As if I had actually been in that other time and the real me wasn't here anymore. If something happened to Pascale when I was there, where would that leave me?"

"What could happen?" Jeff asked.

"She's a ghost, Jeff! Something must have happened—"

"To make her dead!" Molly finished helpfully. She seemed more interested than scared.

"What you said about being caught up in Pascale's memories gives me an idea," Jeff said. His blue eyes were bright with excitement. "If that's all a ghost is—memories—then we could take Pascale's memories on floppy disk over to the Dewey House. It's the electronic-age version of trapping a ghost in a bottle! I bet it would work on a computer ghost."

"We just walk up to the Dewey House and deliver the ghost on a disk?" Sarah asked. "That sounds too easy!"

"We'd have to come up with a way to get invited in, so that we could put the disk somewhere safe," Jeff said. "I'll see if I can talk Mom into visiting Mrs. Gibson. After all, she is a sort of relative of ours."

"How will we know when we have enough memories?" Sarah asked.

"There's probably enough now," Jeff said. "Though

it would be interesting to know what did happen . . .
to turn her into a ghost."

"That's the last thing I want to know!" Sarah said
with an edge of panic in her voice. "Suppose I was
there . . ."

"Then we'd be dealing with two. . . . Sorry!" Jeff
swallowed his words when he saw the look on Sarah's
face.

Washday

That night Sarah lay awake for a long time thinking about Jeff's idea. She wondered if just delivering the disk of memories would be enough. Or did they have to be transferred to someone? Maybe she and Jeff should sell Mrs. Gibson a computer. But surely Pascale would be able to reach Mrs. Gibson without a computer if she wanted to. She'd communicated with people before computers were invented.

Sarah's other worry was that for Jeff's idea to succeed, they needed all the bits and bytes of Pascale's memory that they could save on the disk. She still had the last episode to write up. Sarah didn't mind when Pascale left messages on the computer. In fact, she liked finding out about Pascale that way. What she didn't like was when Pascale and she sort of merged. It was as if Pascale was feeding information into Sarah's head the same way she did into a computer—impulses to her brain cells. Weird! And Sarah worried that while she was plotting ways to get Pascale back to the Dewey House, Pascale might be working on her own plan. Sarah didn't like the idea of that. Even if Pascale didn't mean any harm, she wasn't someone who thought things through. Take the time she'd gone off to collect frog spawn during lunch recess.

From now on, Sarah decided, she was going to stay in control. She'd type the title WASHDAY on the screen and leave it for Pascale to fill in, like an assignment. She wouldn't even wait around for it to happen. She could go over to Denim Blues in the shopping center and look for school clothes. Her mom would probably like that idea.

But when Sarah put her plan into action the next morning, it didn't work the way she expected. Perhaps Pascale had spent the night planning, too. Sarah had only typed the letters w-a-s-h when she saw Pascale's face staring back at her from the screen as if it were her own reflection. Then she heard someone talking in that grating, authoritative voice that was becoming familiar.

"Mr. Jardine and Sam and I are taking the steamboat to Salem to visit the Harrisons, and we'll be gone for two days. With the washing today and ironing tomorrow you and Tibbie will hardly have time to miss us. And be sure you remember to starch the curtains, Pascale."

She looked around and was dismayed to see that the pile of laundry was as tall as she was!

Starch made the curtains hard to iron. She pulled a face behind Maud's back. Even though she was happy that Maud was going away for two days, she didn't see how on earth she and Tibbie could manage all that washing on their own. The wet blankets would be too heavy for them to lift onto the line. More than once Pascale had allowed them to trail in the dirt and then had to wash them all over again, scrubbing the stains on the washboard till her knuckles were raw.

Tibbie, however, was quite cheerful about the whole business.

"Slip on your coat, Pascale, and follow Maud and Alfred down to the boat landing when they leave the house," she whispered. "I've known the steamboat to be hours late. I want to be sure they're safely on it before we carry out my plan."

Pascale eagerly joined the crowds of people heading down to First Street to meet the *Grahamona*. There was always a festive air in Dixon Landing when a steamboat was due. Some people were going aboard and others were meeting friends or picking up supplies. Pascale was keeping well out of sight behind the Witness Tree when she saw Alfred, with Maud on his arm, make his way up the ramp. Poor Sam looked stiff and uncomfortable in his best suit as he followed them onto the deck. The shouting and laughter, the water slapping against the boat, the oily smell of the engine, and the clanging bells brought back the old days when Pascale had traveled with Papa. How she wished he would come! She was old enough now to have a part in the opera. She could be a chorus girl and wear black tights, or even the leading lady, dressed in furs and feathers! She was rather small and skinny, and she didn't have beautiful, thick chestnut hair like Mama, but she did have dancing feet. When she heard music, she couldn't be still. There were times when she couldn't keep from dancing to the music inside her own head.

When Pascale returned home with word that the *Grahamona* had come and gone, Tibbie was in the kitchen with the laundry all heaped together, but she hadn't washed a single thing.

"We're going to take the whole bundle down to the Chinese laundry on Second Street!" she told Pascale. "We'll pick it up tomorrow before the boat comes in. With the curtains hung again and the sheets all in the airing cupboard, nobody's going to be any the wiser."

Pascale's eyes sparkled at the audacity of Tibbie's plan.

"How are you going to pay for it?" she asked.

"There's money in the tea caddy," Tibbie answered. "That money's as much mine as it is Maud's. So let's get the washing down to the laundry and not waste this lovely sunshine on drying clothes!"

They had a wonderful day. They walked up the Willamette to the place where the Mary's River flowed into it, and then they followed the Mary's River to an Indian camping ground.

"The first time I came here was with Maud, when I was very small," Tibbie said. "After Ma died, Maud wouldn't go with me anymore, so I went on my own. Poor Maud always had too much to do, running the house and being a mother to me. She missed out on a lot of fun in those days."

Tibbie had brought along some small presents for the Indians—needles and thread and colored buttons.

"The children I used to play with don't come anymore," she told Pascale. "Only the old ones come back to dig the camas root."

At first Pascale was shy, but Tibbie knew most of the old people by name. They made a great fuss over Pascale, encouraging her to dance and sing. An old wrinkled woman with bright eyes gave her a blue glass bead as a present. It was transparent blue on the outside with a deeper blue spiral around the hole through its middle. Pascale held it up to the sun and thought she'd never seen anything so beautiful in all her life.

"I'll wear it around my neck, and I'll show it to Papa when he comes," she said. "I'll bring him to see you someday. Papa would love it here."

At the end of the afternoon Pascale wished she could stay with the Indians, where life wasn't ruled by washdays and cleaning days and baking days, with no time left for fun. But she couldn't. She had promised Papa she'd be at the Dewey House. She had to go back there to wait for him.

On the way home they stopped in at the laundry on Second Street to make sure that Mr. Lee was remembering to starch the curtains—just enough to give them some body, but not so much as to make them stiff—and to fold the sheets the right way. When Tibbie gave him the instructions he smiled and nodded and bowed, then smiled some more.

Then he said, "What can I do for you, young lady?"

But it wasn't Mr. Lee's voice that asked the question.

He and the laundry were gone. And Tibbie. And Pascale. Sarah was herself again, but she had no idea where she was. She wasn't in the Big Apple. She looked wildly around. She seemed to be in some sort of restaurant. A sign on a chalkboard above the counter in front of her read LEMONADE: 75 CENTS.

"Take your time!"

The words were spoken by a young man in a green apron and held more than a hint of sarcasm.

Digging in her jeans pocket, Sarah came up with a crumpled dollar.

"A glass of lemonade, please," she whispered.

She carried the glass to a table with a checkered cloth. The place seemed vaguely foreign and old-fashioned. But the customers' clothes looked all right—

jeans and shorts and T-shirts. Sarah sipped her lemonade. Even though it eased the dryness in her throat, she set the glass down. She had to get out of here. She couldn't stand not knowing where she was.

The Blue Bead

When Sarah stepped outside, she recognized the post office farther along the street and got her bearings at once. Her knees went weak with relief. She was on Second Street, near the river—only a few blocks from Fifth and Baker. She examined the building she'd just been in. It was called the Old World Center—which accounted for the foreign atmosphere in the restaurant—and it contained several boutiques. They gave the place a contemporary look, though it could have housed a laundry long ago. But Sarah didn't want to deal with that right now. She wanted to get back to the computer store and make sure that everything was all right. She wondered uneasily if Pascale had stayed behind—or had they somehow been together on that day so long ago?

When she reached the shopping plaza, the first person she saw was Jeff Cuff. He was fooling around on the low wall in front of the fountain, wrestling with a boy Sarah didn't know. Ordinarily she wouldn't have rushed up to Jeff and started talking to him when he was with another friend, but this couldn't wait.

"Hey, Jeff!" she shouted.

When he heard his name, Jeff looked up, giving the other boy an advantage. The next instant Jeff was sitting in the fountain.

"Hello!" Sarah said a little uncertainly.

"Do introduce me to your girlfriend!" the boy said, grinning down at Jeff as he struggled to his feet, then slipped on the slimy bottom of the fountain and sat down again.

"Thanks a lot!" Jeff said sarcastically. It wasn't clear whom he was talking to.

"I've got something really important to tell you, Jeff," Sarah persisted.

"Something important!" the other boy echoed, rolling his eyes.

"Okay! Okay! . . . See you at soccer, Brian!"

"I can take a hint," Brian said, and jumped onto his skateboard.

A puddle formed around Jeff's feet as he watched Brian weave across the plaza, dodging shoppers. When Brian was out of sight, Jeff turned to Sarah and asked, "Well?"

Sarah didn't know how to begin. The plaza of a busy shopping center on a hot summer afternoon was not the best setting for telling a ghost story. Nor was Jeff in his present condition an ideal audience.

"I was in her time again," she said slowly. "And

when I came back, I wasn't in the store. I was in the Old World Center down on Second Street."

"You expect me to swallow that?"

"I'm scared, Jeff!" Sarah wailed. "I've got to talk to you."

"And I'm wet," Jeff answered without much show of sympathy. "I can't come into your dad's store like this. If he didn't blow a fuse, one of the computers likely would. Do you want to come over to my place instead? You can bring me up to date on the way."

"Okay," Sarah said. "But I have to let Dad know where I'm going."

"While I stand around and drip dry," Jeff complained.

Sarah dashed into the building and raced up the ramp. Telling her dad that she was going to Jeff's was really an excuse to check the store. She breathed easier when, through the store window, she saw her dad helping a customer while a few people wandered around. All very ordinary.

"Where have you been?" her dad asked as she burst through the door.

"Talking to Jeff out in the plaza," Sarah answered. "I'm going to his house for a little while. Okay?"

"Yes, Sarah, but I do wish you'd remember to turn off the computer when you leave."

"It is off!"

"It's off, because I turned it off!" Mr. Pearce snapped.

"When did you turn it off?" Sarah asked.

"When? I don't see that it matters *when*. It must have been fifteen or twenty minutes ago."

Fifteen or twenty minutes ago . . . just before Sarah ordered lemonade in the Old World Center.

As they walked up Baker Street through the shady tunnel of trees Sarah told Jeff how, back when those same trees were spindly saplings, Pascale had been left to do the washing. Jeff wasn't overly interested. He was in a hurry to reach home and only half listened when Sarah told him about Tibbie and Pascale taking the curtains and bedding to the Chinese laundry. But when she told him about the Indians digging camas root on the banks of the Mary's River and described the blue bead the old Indian woman gave her, she finally got his attention. He stopped and stared at her.

"Go over that again!"

"There were these Indians that Tibbie and Maud used to visit—"

"Not that part," Jeff said impatiently. "About the blue bead. What exactly did it look like?"

"The blue bead?" Sarah wondered if Jeff was making fun of her, but he seemed to be serious, almost anxious.

"It was clear blue glass with a dark spiral in the middle," Sarah said.

For the first time since he'd heard about the ghost, Jeff looked frightened.

"There's no way you could know about that bead," he said slowly. "No way . . . unless Molly showed it to you on Monday."

"Molly?"

"But she couldn't have. I never told her about it."

"What are you talking about, Jeff?"

"I found a bead like that—with a dark blue spiral running through the middle. I wonder if it's the same one."

"There must be other blue beads."

"But I found mine in the Dewey House. It was the day they moved the house. I got bored waiting for them to take down the stoplights at Harrison Street, so I went back up to Fifth to take a look at the hole where the house used to be. I thought it would be a good place to look for old coins—they could have slipped down through the floorboards. The only thing I found was a blue bead. Then this guy yelled that I shouldn't be there, so I ran."

"How come you never told me this before?" Sarah asked.

"I didn't know it mattered."

When Jeff showed Sarah the bead, she recognized it at once.

"I guess I have to believe in Pascale now," Jeff said,

turning the bead over in his hand. "I always thought there was something strange about this bead. I broke out in goose bumps when I picked it up. I felt cold all over, even though it was a hot day."

"So what do we do now?" Sarah asked.

"What we've already decided," Jeff said. "We'll take the disk to the Dewey House. And I know how we can get inside the house! Last night Mom mentioned the historical society's tour of homes. It's on Saturday, and the Dewey House is on the tour. All we need are tickets. Then we wander through the house looking for a good place to hide the disk!"

"Maybe we should take the blue bead as well," Sarah said. "Seeing it was Pascale's."

"No way!" Jeff said. "It's mine now."

"It's Pascale's," Sarah argued.

"Finders keepers!" Jeff retorted, holding the bead out of reach.

Sarah threw herself at Jeff and almost managed to grab the bead, but they were interrupted by the sudden appearance of Molly.

"Have you been playing in the sprinkler, Jeff?" she demanded.

"No," Jeff answered. "I've been swimming in a fountain."

"Mom!" Molly yelled. "Jeff's teasing me! And I get to play in the sprinkler, too!"

The Glorious Fourth

Sarah decided not to go to the Big Apple on Friday, but during breakfast her dad reminded her that she still hadn't finished the handout for the computer club. She promised she'd do it, but then put off going to the store as long as she could. She spent part of the morning watching Jeff's team lose a soccer game. Then she went to the library and inquired at the reference desk if there were any books about the early days in Dixon Landing. She was given a file of pamphlets and clippings. The only article about the Dewey House was recent—a newspaper photograph taken the day the house was moved. After returning the file, she left the library and wandered aimlessly down toward the river.

And all the time the computer store was pulling her like a magnet.

Finally she gave in.

When she reached the Big Apple, she went straight

to the computer second from the window and loaded Applewriter. Maybe if she told Pascale what they were planning to do, Pascale would leave her alone. Sarah typed WE'RE GOING TO TAKE YOU TO THE DEWEY HOUSE TOMORROW. Then she sat back and waited.

She didn't have to wait long.

On the other side of the store a catalog slipped off the counter with a loud crash and the door chime made a rippling sound, almost like laughter, although no one was going out or in.

Mr. Pearce asked no one in particular, "What next?"

Sarah didn't answer. She was reading the words THANK YOU as they appeared on the screen.

Pascale had understood the message!

Sarah printed the handouts and then brought Pascale's memories up to date on the disk. She was convinced that the more memories there were, the better the chance of success. She wished that Jeff had given her the blue bead to take along as well. Something that Pascale had once valued would surely help to anchor her.

"Finders keepers!" was what Jeff had said when he held the bead out of reach.

"Finders keepers, losers weepers!" She could see his teasing eyes, almost as blue as the bead, as he held it just beyond her reach.

For a moment Sarah tried to struggle against what was happening. But her desire for the bead—or Pascale's desire—was too strong.

"It's mine! Give it to me!" she screamed in a shrill, excited voice.

"But I found it! Finders keepers, losers weepers!"

She clawed at his arm, trying to drag it down. Her feet skidded on the loose gravel on the path.

"Do stop teasing the child, Sam!"

Tibbie had been watching the scuffle from the kitchen window.

"That's Pascale's bead right enough," she said, coming to the door. "I was there when the old Indian woman gave it to her."

Sam sent the bead flying over Pascale's head. She saw where it landed and went down on her knees in the grass looking for it. A loud bang brought her back to her feet, but she had the bead clenched in her fist.

"What was that noise?" she asked.

"The gun salute welcoming in the Glorious Fourth!" Tibbie said. "Do come inside and I'll finish fixing the dress for you."

"So I can be in the parade with Billy pulling the cart!" Pascale said, bouncing up and down with excitement.

"I'll only let you if you give me back that bead," Sam said.

"But you said I could . . ."

"Stop teasing her, Sam," Tibbie said sternly. "She gets excited enough on her own without you adding to it! Come along, Pascale, and I'll help you get dressed. Otherwise you'll not be in the parade—bead or no bead!"

Pascale could hardly stand still while Tibbie pinned and stitched the red-and-white-striped dress with a wide blue collar decorated with white stars. Tibbie had worn the dress when she was twelve, so it was too long for Pascale and needed a tuck here and there. But she loved it. When Tibbie was at last finished, Pascale twirled around and the skirt billowed out.

"I'll string your bead on this satin ribbon so you can wear it around your neck."

"Thank you, Tibbie!"

Pascale could hear Sam and his friend John shouting and laughing down in the yard while they scrubbed the Angora goat. What a wonderful morning to be alive!

When Pascale went racing outside to show off the dress, Sam grinned at her. "You look nice!" he said. "You and my old goat'll be the best entry in Dixon Landing, and that's for sure!"

The cart, painted red, white, and blue, stood ready. Other years Sam had ridden in it, but now he was too gangly. Skipping around in Tibbie's old dress, Pascale knew she'd look much better in the parade than Sam ever had.

She loved every minute of it. The cheering crowds made her feel like a princess. Or as if she were on-stage. She waved and laughed, but then Billy spied a wheelbarrow filled with fresh flowers and decided it was time for lunch. A tall Swede with long blond hair and outlandish clothes of fur and leather saved them from disaster and disgrace. He told Pascale his name was Lars Erikson.

Later, down by the ferry landing, Pascale danced with Lars to the music of the town band. They danced well together—he so tall and blond, Pascale so small and dark. People formed a circle around them, clapping and tapping their feet, cheering them on. When the music ended, Pascale dragged Lars over to meet Tibbie, and that was the end of her dancing with Lars. He and Tibbie danced together until the last light faded from the western sky.

Meantime Pascale and Sam walked back to the Dewey House, too tired even to spar with each other. Before Pascale climbed into bed, she crossed the room and looked out the window, just as she did every single night.

The window merged with the computer screen and Sarah blinked, as if she half expected to see stars in the night sky. So Lars was Tibbie's beau, she thought. Then she quickly corrected the word in her mind to "boyfriend." It was easy to see why Alfred and Maud Jardine wouldn't approve of Lars—the way he dressed in such rough clothes. But Sarah knew why Tibbie had fallen in love with him.

13

The Historic Homes
Tour

On Saturday morning Beth Cohen and Les Metzgar both asked Sarah how things were going. In fact, most of the computer club kids spoke to her, but she was so busy wondering what could have happened to Jeff that she hardly answered. The historic homes tour was supposed to get underway with a speech by the mayor at ten o'clock in the plaza. Jeff had said he'd see Sarah at the Big Apple and they could go from there.

He finally showed up at nine forty-five, with Molly in tow.

"I have to look after Molly this morning," he explained. "The only way Mom would let me go on the tour was if I brought Molly along. Mom seemed to think my sudden interest in old houses was just to get out of baby-sitting. It isn't fair!"

"The main thing is that you're here," Sarah said. "Molly won't be any trouble."

"Can I see Pascale?" Molly asked, looking around the store, wide-eyed.

"Hush!" Sarah and Jeff said together.

"Let's get her out of here," Jeff added.

Sarah wasn't sure if he meant Molly or Pascale. She reached for the disk containing Pascale's memories and slipped it into the bag she'd brought.

"I'm ready!" she said.

Sarah and Jeff climbed up on the low wall around the fountain, with Molly between them, to listen to Mayor Wilson's speech. He began by telling about the granting of a charter to Dixon Landing back in 1857. It sounded as if it was going to be a long speech. Molly stuck a toe in the water and Sarah grabbed her to steady her. When the mayor mentioned Daniel Dewey, who had struck it rich in the California Gold Rush of 1848 and then come to Oregon to spend his money, Sarah began to listen again. But her mind wandered when he began to ramble on abut Dixon Landing preserving its past while moving into the future. His last words—something about the shuttle buses lined up on Fifth Street giving free rides to the historic homes—were lost in a mad rush to board the buses.

Sarah and Jeff found themselves quite far back in the crowd, but Molly managed to squirm her way into the first bus.

"There'll be another along in a few minutes," the driver said, barring the doorway.

"Hey! My little sister's in there!" Jeff shouted.

People let them through, and the driver told them, quite good-naturedly, to hop aboard. Sarah, red-faced with embarrassment, clutched her bag and squeezed into the crowded bus.

The bus headed over to Second Street, then turning right off Second trundled along Pioneer Lane to the Willamette River. When they came to a stop at the end of the road, Sarah saw the house nestled against two old sycamore trees. For a moment she wondered if it could really be the Dewey House—it looked as if it had always been there. Red and yellow snapdragons and white petunias hid the new foundations. A wide lawn sprinkled with daisies and dandelions and cornflowers sloped toward the river. But the porch and gables were right, when you took into account that the house had been placed to look out at the curve of the river instead of onto the street.

"Hasn't she done a great job of fixing it up?" Jeff asked. "Though of course you wouldn't know, never having seen it before."

"But I have!" Sarah pointed out.

"Oh, yeah!" Jeff said. "I'd almost forgotten why we'd come."

"Pascale's going to feel right at home here," Sarah said, patting her bag.

People spilled off the bus and streamed up the steps to the veranda. Sarah and Jeff wanted to hang back, so as not to be part of the crowd, but they had to keep up with Molly.

Inside the house the sun, shining through narrow stained-glass panels on either side of the front door, made an overlay of color on the patterned carpet. The hallway was papered in gold and hung with pictures. Sarah tried to get a closer look at the photographs, but a woman hurried them into the sitting room. It was crammed with people and armchairs and lamps and little tables covered with ornaments and still more photographs.

In the dining room one of the ladies from the historical society gave a talk about the furniture. She pointed out an old dresser that had come over the Oregon Trail in 1850. "Far more pieces of furniture were abandoned on the trail than ever made it to Oregon," she said. "Some were lost fording rivers, some chopped up for firewood on the prairies, but most were abandoned when the oxen grew too weak to pull the load and the weary pioneers had to continue on foot."

"We could slip the disk into one of those drawers," Sarah whispered. "That would be a far better place for a ghost than a disk drive."

"How are you going to get it there?" Jeff asked.

Sarah looked at the stern woman standing between her and the dresser and decided it wasn't such a great idea after all. They followed the crowd through the kitchen and then upstairs, where only the front bedrooms were open to the public. A sign across the landing warned visitors that the back bedrooms were not part of the tour.

"Where's Molly?" Jeff asked suddenly.

"She was here a moment ago," Sarah answered, looking around. The crowd had thinned somewhat.

"I bet she's outside having punch and cookies. You can always count on Molly to be the first in line for cookies. I'll go down and see if I can find her."

"Okay! And I'll wait here in case she comes back to look for us," Sarah offered.

Gradually everyone else went downstairs, leaving the upstairs room very quiet. Then the silence was broken by a thin voice singing words that were all too familiar: "Please won't you be my neighbor?" The singing seemed to come from one of the back rooms.

Just then Jeff came back, out of breath and looking worried. "She's not downstairs and she's not in the cookie line," he said. "I can't find her anywhere."

"Listen!" Sarah said.

They tiptoed along the upstairs landing, ignoring the sign. Jeff pushed open the last door on the left. Looking past him, Sarah took in the flowered wallpaper and the brass bedstead with a patchwork quilt. And in the corner, holding a doll in her lap and rocking quietly, sat a little pale-faced girl.

Sarah let out her breath with a loud sigh. "It's just Molly!" she said. "For a moment I thought it was Pascale. But this is her room. It's exactly the way it was when I saw it."

"Then this must be Pansy," Jeff said, carefully taking the china-faced doll from Molly and laying it on the bed. "You shouldn't be in here, Molly! But you have led us to the perfect place to leave the disk."

"How did all her furniture get here?" Sarah asked. "The room wasn't like this when those students lived here."

"Mrs. Gibson bought a lot of the Dewey House furniture back in the sixties when Danny Jardine died and the city took the place over," Jeff said. "She had some of it in her other house and some in storage. I guess she's been planning for years to bring the house and the furniture together again. I'm glad she got the chance."

"So am I," Sarah said.

The sound of voices on the stairs reminded them that they shouldn't be in the back room. Sarah hurriedly slipped the disk into the top drawer of the dresser, whispering, "You're home, Pascale! Back in the Dewey House where you belong!"

They scampered back along the corridor without being seen.

"Which one's Mrs. Gibson?" Sarah asked a few minutes later when they were eating cookies in the garden.

There seemed to be an abundance of old women in flowery dresses, any one of whom might have been the lady of the house.

"I dunno," Jeff said. He seemed a little uncomfortable being part of the historical tour now that they had deposited the ghost. "Let's walk back into town and skip the rest of the houses."

The Dewey House, in spite of its peaceful surroundings, wasn't far from downtown, though the walk back took a long time because Molly had to examine so many things along the way.

"She's like Pascale on her way to school," Sarah said. "Picking stones out of the gutter and putting caterpillars in her shorts pockets."

Even though Sarah was glad for Pascale's sake— and for the computer store's sake—that they'd delivered the ghost, she was going to miss her. She hoped Mrs. Gibson wouldn't mind having the little ghost in Pascale's room. Pascale hadn't caused any trouble most of the time. She seemed only to bother people when she was unhappy about the house. But she'd be content now, with her room exactly the way it was long ago. "Nicer than any room I'd ever been in before," she'd said.

Sarah was glad they'd been able to help Pascale, because Pascale had helped her. Already Dixon

Landing felt like home. Thanks to Pascale, Sarah was beginning to know her way around the town. And she had friends—Jeff and Molly, and even the other computer club kids. Yesterday, watching the soccer game, some girls had talked to her. She wasn't invisible anymore!

When they reached the Dewey Shopping Plaza, they stopped in at the Big Apple.

"How was the history tour?" Mr. Pearce asked.

"It was great!" Sarah answered. "How are things here?"

"Quiet," her dad said. "Really quiet!"

The store was quieter than usual. A calm, peaceful sort of quiet.

14

The Computer Store

When Sarah awakened the next morning, the sun was streaming through the slats of the venetian blinds on her bedroom window, making a pattern across her bed and on the thick blue carpet on the floor. She lay in bed, feeling good. She could smell coffee . . . and blueberry muffins. She heard the rustle of the Sunday papers and a soft exchange of voices every now and then when her mom and dad commented on something in the news. Pretty soon they'd be leaving for church. They were trying out different churches and had agreed that Sarah could wait till they'd narrowed it down before she had to go. An hour or so later she had the house and the funny papers to herself. The good feeling was still there. Then suddenly the phone rang. It sounded loud and persistent, almost like a warning. She grabbed the receiver.

"Sarah, it's me!"

"Who?"

"Me—Jeff!"

He was so out of breath that he didn't sound like himself.

"What's wrong?" Sarah asked.

"It didn't work, Sarah. Taking her to the Dewey House didn't work. In fact, I think it made her mad or something."

"How can you tell?" Sarah asked. The good feeling had completely vanished. She felt cold and slightly sick.

"I was down at the Double Scoop with Molly, and I looked across at your dad's store. Every computer in the whole place is lit up, flashing messages on and off. It's a wonder the fuses haven't blown."

"So Pascale's come back?"

"Or she never left."

"What's made her so angry?"

"Maybe because you told her she was going home—"

"And then your great idea didn't work."

"I've been thinking about what could have gone wrong," Jeff said. "Maybe someone has to receive the memories from the disk. If we could just sell Mrs. Gibson a computer—"

"Sell Mrs. Gibson a computer!" Sarah snapped. "By the time we did that, Dad wouldn't have any computers to sell! We have to do something now."

"Such as?"

"When Dad comes home from church, I'm going to tell him everything."

"He'll think you're putting him on if you tell him about Pascale," Jeff said. "And he'll blame us for turning on all the computers."

"What else can I do?"

"Do you have a key to the store?" Jeff asked.

"There's a spare one right here on the bulletin board by the phone. Why?"

"I think you should go in and unplug the machines before Pascale ruins all that electronic equipment."

"Are you phoning from the plaza, Jeff?"

"No! I'm at home—I had to bring Molly back here."

"Will you come down and help me?" Sarah asked.

"I'd just as soon be able to say I hadn't been any-where near the place in case Pascale's already wrecked everything."

"Jeff!" Sarah wailed.

"Okay, I'll come."

"Thanks," Sarah said. "I'll see you down there."

"If I ride my bike, we should get there about the same time," Jeff answered.

As it turned out, Sarah reached the computer store first. The monitors were glowing fiercely. Some had words flickering across the screen: HELP ME FIND MY WAY HOME and TAKE ME BACK TO THE DEWEY HOUSE. Others had flashing designs, and a few had outlines of a house.

Sarah was so alarmed by the intensity of the light on the screens that she decided she didn't dare wait for Jeff. She unlocked the door and rushed in, switching off each computer in turn. By the time she reached her computer, the one second from the window, the screen was blank. Though not completely blank. A face was looking out from the monitor. Sarah looked at her reflection—bangs across her forehead, shoulder-length hair, with her ears showing through. She felt herself grow cold as she watched her face gradually change. Today it was Pascale's turn. Pascale had her own plan, and Sarah couldn't pull herself away.

When Jeff arrived at the Big Apple, he was completely out of breath. He'd had to stop to put air in one of his tires and then had cycled fast to make up for lost time. The first thing he noticed was that the door was open and the key was still in the lock. All the machines except the second one from the window were turned off. And there wasn't a soul around. No one.

"Sarah!" Jeff called.

No answer.

He checked the storeroom behind the counter.

No one.

"Sarah!"

He crossed over to the computer second from the window. A face was looking at him from the monitor. He couldn't make out who it was, because the outline was blurry, almost as if he were seeing it through water.

He reached over and switched off the computer. The face disappeared. Not knowing what else to do, he went out of the store, closing the door behind him and turning the key in the lock.

15

Tibbie and Lars

Her eyes locked with Tibbie's for a second, but then she looked down quickly at her plate. Nothing must give away the fact that this was the last breakfast Tibbie would eat with them. Pascale was both excited and sad, her feelings all mixed up like the sharpness of the huckleberry jam and the warm, comforting taste of the fresh bread she was chewing. Lars and Tibbie were going to elope! They were taking the steamboat downriver to Salem, where they would get married.

These last few weeks had been filled with secrets and romance! All the scheming and planning so that Tibbie and Lars could meet without Maud knowing. Pascale had kept a lookout for Lars coming across the river on the ferry, and then she wrote notes arranging where he and Tibbie were to meet. Pascale always wrote down exactly what Lars told her to, except for the time she added love and kisses. Tibbie had blushed scarlet when she read that note!

That was the morning Maud had nearly caught

them. Soon after Tibbie had gone down to the Witness Tree by the river to meet Lars, Maud had complained that it was so stiflingly hot that she was going to walk down to the ferry landing to get a breath of fresh air. When Pascale heard where Maud was going, she gave a jug of milk sitting near the edge of the sideboard a slight nudge that sent it crashing to the floor. It was such a pretty blue-and-white-striped jug that she was sorry to see it lying there in so many pieces. Maud was sorry, too. She slapped Pascale hard and then scolded her for close to thirty minutes. When Maud finally left the house, she went in the direction of the dairy to buy more milk instead of going down to the river.

Later, when Tibbie came home singing to herself, Pascale thought it was surely worth a broken jug, a few slaps, and a scolding.

But now Tibbie and Lars were going to live in Lars's cabin in the mountains and would only come back to Dixon Landing now and again when Lars had pelts to trade for supplies. Tibbie had wanted Pascale to go with them, but she'd understood when Pascale said she couldn't. She'd promised to wait for Papa. If she wasn't at the Dewey House when Papa came back, he might not be able to find her.

When breakfast was finished, it was up to Pascale to make the plan work. Alfred had gone off to the hardware store and now Maud was gathering together the ingredients to make a cake for supper.

"We seem to be out of baking powder," Pascale said innocently. The tin was empty because she had just that moment tipped it into the flour bin. "I'll run down to the grocer and buy some more," she offered. "I'll go straight there and back."

"I'll go myself," Maud said, peering suspiciously into the tin. "I've never known you to go straight there and back to anywhere."

Pascale had been sure that that would be the answer. If she hadn't offered to go, Maud would probably have sent her! Humming to herself, she fetched an armload of firewood, while Maud fixed her hair at the small speckled kitchen mirror and then pinned her hat firmly on her head.

"I'll only be gone a few minutes," Maud promised.

No sooner had she left than Pascale dashed out of the house in the opposite direction and raced down to the Occidental Hotel in search of Lars. He was lounging around outside. His golden hair made him easy to find.

"Lars! Lars!" Pascale called out breathlessly. "Maud's over at the grocer's. We've hidden Tibbie's trunk in the garden shed, and you must come right away to take it down to the boat landing. Tibbie can't manage it on her own."

After Lars had picked up the trunk, Pascale watched the kitchen clock as anxiously as Tibbie. The steamboat was to leave at one. Tibbie, her face hidden by Maud's heavy veil, was going to slip aboard just before it left. Lars would be waiting on board—they didn't want to be seen going on the *Grahamona* together.

Fate was with them. Maud had been invited to lunch with the Olsens, and that meant Pascale would be free to go down to the boat landing to see them off. The riverbank was always crowded when the steamboat docked. Today barking dogs and snuffling pigs and cages of cackling hens all added to the pandemonium. Pascale squirmed through the crowd in search of Tibbie, so that she could say good-bye one more time. She almost jumped out of her skin when she saw Alfred Jardine. The hardware store closed for an hour at lunchtime, but neither Pascale nor Tibbie had expected Alfred to show up here. He always went to the Occidental Hotel for lunch when Maud wasn't home, yet here he was on the wharf, talking to the steamboat engineer. If he stayed where he was, he'd see Tibbie going on board. He'd recognize her for sure. The veil wasn't much of a disguise—not when it belonged to his own wife!

"You don't need to shut the engine right down," Alfred was telling the engineer. "Keep up a head of steam. It'll only take me a few minutes to fetch a new valve from my workshop. I'm sure I have something that'll work."

Alfred pushed through the crowd. He waved to his competitor Isaac Smith. Isaac was setting up a shop on Third Street. Maud didn't care for him, but Alfred was sure that as more people got those new automobiles there would be more than enough work for both of them.

Pascale's heart missed a beat when she heard Isaac shout, "Is that pretty sister-in-law of yours taking off on a trip?"

"I reckon not," Alfred said, and hurried on.

Pascale shadowed him, wondering how she could delay him until the steamboat was gone. He turned down an alley on Fourth Street, next to his hardware store. He was apparently heading for his machine shop, where he liked to tinker with engines whenever he got the chance. Pascale followed. The alley was littered with crates and boxes, so it was easy to keep out of sight, dodging from one crate to the next. If Alfred did see her, she was ready to say that she had a message from Maud, but he was in a great hurry and didn't once look back. Instead of going into the machine shop, however, he unlocked the door of a small windowless shed next to it. Leaving the door ajar and the key in the lock, Alfred stepped in and reached for a box labeled VALVES. Pascale leaped forward, slammed the door shut, and turned the key before Alfred could even turn around. She jerked the key out of the lock and hurled it into a blackberry thicket. With the hardware store closed for lunch and everyone down at the river, no one would hear Alfred hollering for help.

Pascale hung around for a while, just to make sure that her prisoner didn't escape, and then went back to the steamboat feeling very pleased with herself. The boat should be leaving soon. She looked everywhere for Tibbie, but she couldn't see her. Of course, Tibbie would be keeping out of sight till they were on their way.

Feeling a bit let down after so much excitement, Pascale left the crowded landing and took the path along the river's edge. She hated the idea of Tibbie going away without saying good-bye properly. But if she followed along the bank to the meadow at the bend where the river turned east, she'd see the big sternwheeler go past. Maybe Tibbie would be on the deck and Pascale could wave to her one last time.

When she came to the meadow, she scrambled down through the bushes to the river's edge to get a clear view. At that moment a sound louder than all the guns shooting off to welcome the Fourth of July shattered the silence. There was screaming, too. Coming from upriver where the sternwheeler was. And smoke and more shouting. Pascale's heart began to pound. The steam engine must have blown up! And as if the explosion had blown the mist from her brain, she suddenly understood why it had happened. The little valve Alfred had gone to fetch was to let the steam escape. And she had locked him in the shed, so he hadn't gotten it back in time.

Pascale stared at the swift, smooth water of the Willamette River. To her horror she saw that things were floating down it—bits of the boat. A life buoy with no one hanging on to it, a red cushion—and a black bonnet. That was Tibbie's hat, she was sure of it! She plunged into the river and tried to grab the hat, as if by doing so she could save poor, dear Tibbie. But the water was deep and the current was strong. The next moment she was fighting for her own life, choking, coughing, struggling . . .

16

Mrs. Gibson

As soon as her breathing became less labored and her panic eased, she began to notice other aches and pains. Her right arm felt as if it had been jerked out of its socket and her left knee was throbbing. Also, she was soaking wet. Her feet were squelching inside her running shoes and her hair was plastered against her head.

Everything around her was half-strange, half-familiar. She was sitting in the big armchair in the kitchen of the Dewey House, but the stove didn't look quite right. Nor did the window over the sink. A huge tree, which shouldn't have been there, was blocking out most of the light. Then something clicked into place in her mind. This was the Dewey House, all right—but the house was in its present-day setting against the sycamore trees at the end of Pioneer Lane. The stove and the sink were modern. And the woman who was fussing over her must be Thelma Gibson. She was a tall, rather severe woman with silvery gray hair pulled back from her face. She looked more like Maud than

Tibbie, but maybe that was because she was tall and was wearing a blue shirt. Maud had always favored blue.

But how had she ended up here? Sarah wondered.

The answer came in a horrifying rush of memories. Pascale locking Alfred in the shed . . . the steamboat blowing up . . . falling into the river and not knowing how to swim.

"She very nearly drowned me!" Sarah said aloud. "Just so she could find the Dewey House. She made it happen all over again. She used me to get back into the house here by the river. . . . She didn't care that I could have drowned. . . ."

"Who are you talking about?" Mrs. Gibson asked, frowning. "Are you saying that someone pushed you in? I didn't see anyone down at the river with you."

"No . . . no, I don't suppose you would. And no one pushed me."

"Why don't you get out of those wet things so I can stick them in the dryer," Mrs. Gibson said, handing Sarah an awful purple bathrobe. As she watched Sarah strip off her jeans and shirt she added, "You're a much bigger girl than I thought!"

Sarah clutched the bathrobe around her, but her embarrassment was forgotten when Mrs. Gibson continued. "I could swear that when I pulled you out of the river you were just a little thing, as skinny and light-boned as a bird. And dark-haired, too! I don't know where I got the strength to drag you up the bank! And I must say it was a lot harder reviving you than working on that dummy we practiced on in the first aid class—blowing into your mouth, with you spitting and coughing."

"Did you really do that?"

"Don't you remember?"

Sarah shook her head. "I'm lucky you knew what to do . . ."

"You don't move a hundred-year-old house without learning to cope with emergencies," Mrs. Gibson said. "But looking at you now, I'm still surprised I carried you back to the house."

"That wasn't me!" Sarah blurted out. "It was Pascale!"

"Pascale!" Mrs. Gibson repeated. "The little ghost?"

"She's come back here . . . to wait for her father."

Sarah owed Mrs. Gibson the truth. After all, she'd saved her life!

"Pascale—that's who you reminded me of!" Mrs. Gibson said. "Though now that I look at you, I can see that you're not a bit like her."

"Did you know Pascale?" Sarah asked.

"My mother had a picture of her, taken at a Fourth of July parade," Mrs. Gibson answered. "She was marching alongside my father in the band."

"Was your father Lars Erikson?" Sarah asked.

Mrs. Gibson nodded.

"The strange thing about that picture was that it was taken in 1912, several years after Pascale disappeared. No one could recall seeing her when the picture was taken, yet there she was when the print was developed, looking not a day older than people remembered her. I suppose that's what started the rumors that the Dewey House was haunted. That, and the fact that no one had a good word to say about Alfred Jardine after the steamboat accident. There was a lot of vicious talk about Alfred blowing up the boat to stop my mother from eloping and Pascale drowning as a result. Though they never did find her body."

"Isaac Smith probably started the rumor about Alfred and Tibbie," Sarah said. "He'd seen her on the boat. But the accident wasn't Alfred's fault. Pascale locked him in the shed so he wouldn't come back and stop Tibbie from leaving."

"How can you possibly know that?" Mrs. Gibson asked.

"From Pascale! And then, when the boat blew up and there was all this debris floating down the river, Pascale saw Tibbie's black bonnet and panicked. She jumped in . . . but she couldn't swim . . . it was awful!"

"So poor little Pascale did drown," Mrs. Gibson said. "And Uncle Alfred had nothing to do with it."

They were interrupted by the doorbell. When Mrs. Gibson went off to answer it, Sarah leaned back in her chair, thinking how different Thelma Gibson was from most grownups. She was open to believing that anything could happen. Sarah figured it was because the old woman wasn't full of doubts and questions that she'd been able to buy the Dewey House and move it. She and Pascale would get along fine.

Sarah heard heavy footsteps approaching down the hallway. She clutched the purple bathrobe around herself when a tall, helmeted fireman walked into the kitchen.

"This is the emergency?" he asked, frowning down at Sarah.

"Why the fire department?" Sarah gasped. Having a fire hose turned on her was the last thing she needed.

"I got them when I dialed 911," Mrs. Gibson explained. "I had to tell someone I'd fished you out of the river."

"What's her name?" the fireman asked, turning to Mrs. Gibson. He didn't seem to think Sarah could speak for herself.

"I never thought to ask," Mrs. Gibson confessed. "We had more important things to talk about."

"We need a name so we can get in touch with her folks," the man said impatiently.

"It would surely alarm them less if she called them herself," Mrs. Gibson pointed out.

But when Sarah called home, no one answered.

"I guess they must still be in church," she said. She was puzzled, because she was sure it was hours since she had left home.

"Where do they go?" the fireman asked.

"I don't know," Sarah admitted. "We're new here,

and they've been going to different churches. I just hope we don't end up at today's one. The preacher must be dreadfully long-winded." But when she looked at the clock, she saw that it wasn't quite noon. It hadn't been so long after all.

The fireman asked a few more questions, most of which Mrs. Gibson found provoking.

No sooner had she shown him out than the doorbell rang again. This time Mrs. Gibson returned with Jeff.

"How did you get here?" Sarah shrieked.

"I could ask you the same question!"

"I nearly drowned, Jeff! If Mrs. Gibson hadn't pulled me out of the river, I would have died."

"You fell in the river?"

"Pascale fell in . . . that's how she died."

"And you were in her time when it happened?"

"Yeah." Sarah nodded. "She used me to bring her to the Dewey House. But how did you know where to find me?"

"When I arrived at the Big Apple, I could tell you'd already been there because the store was unlocked and the computers were turned off," Jeff explained. "All except the one you usually use. And then I saw a face reflected in the monitor. It looked like you, only blurry—as if you were under water—so I switched it off . . ."

"You switched it off . . . and that's when I came

back here! Oh, Jeff! What if you had been a few minutes later?"

They stared at each other, frightened by all that
Sarah's words implied.

"I didn't know what to do next," Jeff said. "I got
on my bike and went down Fifth, hoping I'd see you.
When I was outside the fire station the siren went off.
Then I heard someone saying something about the
Dewey House on a two-way radio, so I came over
here."

Mrs. Gibson insisted that what they all needed was a
good strong cup of tea. By the time they'd finished,
Sarah's clothes were dry, and her parents were home
from church. When they heard that she'd fallen into
the Willamette and was now in the Dewey House,
they told her to stay right there—that they'd come
straight over.

The Pearces arrived bursting with questions. They
weren't accepting listeners like Mrs. Gibson, so Sarah
didn't tell them everything. In fact, she didn't tell them
very much—just that she'd been walking along the
riverbank and had slipped.

"But you're such a strong swimmer, Sarah," her
mom kept saying.

"I guess I panicked a little," Sarah admitted.

"What were you and Jeff doing out here at the
Dewey House?" Mr. Pearce asked. "I thought you came

here yesterday. Or did you leave something behind?"

"Actually, we tried to," Sarah answered. "Though it didn't work out. And Jeff wasn't there when I fell in the river. He came because he heard the fire engine."

"Where was the fire?" Sarah's mom asked, looking bewildered.

"I understand that you sell computers, Mr. Pearce," Mrs. Gibson broke in. Sarah suspected her of trying to change the subject. "I'll have to visit your store one of these days," she continued. "I'm writing a book about the Dewey House, and everyone says it would go much quicker with a word processor."

"I'd be glad to show you our computers," Mr. Pearce said, relieved to be on safe ground. "No writer should be without one."

As they were leaving, Mrs. Gibson told Sarah and Jeff that her grandchildren were coming for a visit the following week. "I do hope you'll both come over and meet them," Mrs. Gibson said.

Jeff and Sarah exchanged glances. It would be good to have an excuse to drop by the Dewey House—to see how Pascale was settling in.

Postscript

On Halloween night Sarah, Molly, Jeff, and his friend Brian turned in their UNICEF boxes at the Double Scoop and received free licorice and orange double scoops as a reward for trick-or-treating for UNICEF. Now they were waiting in the plaza for Jeff's dad to give them a ride home. Sarah was hoping he'd show up soon. She shouldn't have eaten that second double scoop—not on top of all that Halloween candy.

"Hey, Sarah, look at this!" Jeff said. He was pointing to a display in the window of the Book Nook. "It's Mrs. Gibson's book! *House of Memories* by Thelma Gibson."

"Neat!" Sarah said, looking at the photograph of the old house on the cover.

Two other kids came over to look.

"Do you know her?" one of them asked.

"Sure," Sarah said. "Jeff and I played softball with her grandkids last summer. And she bought a computer from our store."

"She really likes the computer," Jeff said.

"Yeah, she claims the book practically wrote it-self!" Sarah added.

Jeff laughed. No one else seemed to find Sarah's answer particularly funny.

"Here's your dad!" Brian said as a car drew up at the curb.

"Where's Molly gone off to now?" Jeff asked impatiently. She was hard enough to keep track of in daylight. It wasn't fair to expect him to look after her on Halloween.

"I see her—over there, by the street," Sarah said.

Molly was wearing a bunny outfit Mrs. Cuff had made for her ballet recital back in the summer—floppy ears and a tutu. She was standing on the sidewalk on the corner of Fifth and Baker with her head thrown back and one arm pointing toward the river. A sort of ballet pose. Or maybe as if she were looking up at someone tall and showing him the way. But there was no one else there.

"Molly! You're keeping everyone waiting!" Jeff yelled. "Don't stand there talking to yourself!"

"I wasn't talking to myself," Molly said when she was close enough for them to hear. "I was talking to a man. He was French. He called me 'mon petit chou.' "

One of the kids gave Molly a short don't-talk-to-strangers lecture, which didn't make sense if Molly hadn't really been talking to anyone.

"He wasn't a stranger," Molly said, pouting. "Even though I hadn't seen him before, I knew who he was. He was looking for the Dewey House and he said it should be on Fifth Street. He was really surprised when I told him they'd moved it. But he'll find it okay. He's come all the way from San Francisco and he's not going to give up now."

"When did he start out?" Brian asked.

"Right after the earthquake," Molly answered.

Sarah wondered which earthquake Molly meant. But that wasn't what mattered. The important thing was that he had come.

Pascale's long wait was finally over.

MARGARET J. ANDERSON, a native of Scotland, graduated from the University of Edinburgh with honors in genetics. She has worked as a biologist, a statistician, and a writer in England, Canada, and the United States. She is the author of many novels for young readers, including *The Druid's Gift*, the award-winning *In the Circle of Time*, and *Searching for Shona*.

Ms. Anderson lives in Corvallis, Oregon, with her husband and four children.

They traded identities—and altered their destinies forever!

SEARCHING FOR SHONA

A story of adventure and mystery by award-winning author
Margaret J. Anderson

It's the start of World War II, and shy, wealthy Marjorie
Malcolm-Scott is about to be evacuated from Edinburgh.
Then, in the midst of the crowded train station she spots
a casual acquaintance, a girl named Shona. The two come
up with a brilliant scheme—they exchange identities,
promising to switch back at the end of the war. In the
blink of an eye, Shona is off to Canada and Marjorie's rich
family, while Marjorie is packed off to the country with
Shona's rather meager possessions—including the only clue
to Shona's true ancestry. As the war drags on, Marjorie
finds happiness in her new life and devotes her time to
unraveling the mystery of Shona's past. But the most com-
pelling mystery of all is this: who *is* the real Shona after
years have gone by? And what if she doesn't want to switch
back?

"Anderson's simple, stark prose is most expressive."
—*School Library Journal*

"Cleverly conceived."   —*Booklist*

Bullseye Books published by Alfred A. Knopf, Inc.

It's not just kid stuff. . . .

WHO STOLE
THE WIZARD OF OZ?

by Avi

When a rare edition of the children's classic *The Wizard of Oz* is found missing from the Checkertown library, the librarian accuses Becky. Boy, is Becky mad! She knows she's innocent, but nobody will believe her. So with the help of her twin brother, Toby, Becky sets out to find the real culprit—and clear her name! But the search turns out to be more than the twins bargained for when they find themselves involved in a full-fledged mystery centered around not just one but *five* missing children's books! Piecing together the clues that they find hidden within the stories, the twins find themselves in a race against time to find the hidden treasure—but can they get to it before the thief does?

"Plenty of action . . ."
—*Bulletin of the Center for Children's Books*

"This is fun reading!"   —*School Library Journal*

Bullseye Books published by Alfred A. Knopf, Inc.